SHANE'S BRIDE

MAIL ORDER BRIDES OF TEXAS BOOK THREE

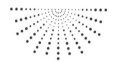

KATHLEEN BALL

This book is dedicated to Edmund Rauschuber. He made it possible for me to type again- Thank you!!
To Jean Joachim and Vicki Locey for telling me I can write a book without using my hands.
To the wonderful readers and authors on the Pioneer Hearts Facebook group. You encouragement made a huge difference.
And to Bruce, Steven, Colt and Clara because I love them.

CHAPTER ONE

$\mathcal{S}$hane O'Connor swung down off his horse, Jester, and patted its back flank before looking at the hoof. Just as he suspected Jester had a rock wedged deep. "It's going to be just fine, boy." He dug out the rock with his pocket knife and watched the paint walk. Damn, the poor horse was limping. "We'll just take it nice and slow." Taking off his hat, Shane wiped his brow with his shirt sleeve, while squinting his eyes at the glaring sun. It must be well past noon. He'd have a long walk before he reached town, if he went back.

Sighing, he shook his head. "I don't know about you, Jester, but I'm tired of chasing down that dang blamed woman and dragging her back to town only to have her run off again." This was the third time and he'd had it. If she wanted to be gone, let her.

Turning the horse south, he began his long walk home. It wasn't his fault if Cecily McGuinness didn't have enough smarts to come in out of the wilderness. He'd done his job and more. He'd rescued her from that big Indian, Long Nose, and every time she ran off, he found her and brought her back. It wasn't as though she liked living with Long Nose. Besides, he was dead. She'd clung to him the whole way back to town and he couldn't figure out why she kept leaving.

Other than being in Texas for a month, he didn't know much about her except she came west as a mail order bride for the unscrupulous John Hardy, who'd tricked many women into coming to Texas. Upon their arrival he'd renege on his marriage proposal and offered them job at his saloon instead. Putting that piece of garbage behind bars had been a pleasure.

Out the corner of his eye he caught a glimpse of rich sable hair. *What the blazes?* She was following him. His lips twitched as he tried to contain his laughter. He'd never figure women out, and he didn't even want to try, they were too much trouble.

"Are you going to follow me all the way back to town?" He kept walking without looking back, leading Jester at a slow pace. She must have stepped on every twig in her path. "You might as well walk with me. It gets boring being all alone." He stopped and listened. The sound of footsteps on dry earth grew louder. She was getting closer. "Don't you get scared in these woods at night? There are bears and mountain lions. Oh, and I forgot to mention the snakes. You don't have a gun do you?" She didn't answer him. He walked for another hour before stopping at a creek.

"Jester, you need some rest, ole buddy." Usually he brought two horses with him, but he'd been on his way to his friend Keegan's ranch, when another friend, Cookie caught up to him to report her missing. He lifted the saddle off Jester and led him to the water, making sure his hurt foot was fully submerged. Hopefully the cold water would help him some. Filling his canteen, he took a healthy swig, pretending all the while Cecily wasn't behind the big oak tree. Could be she'd come and sit by him. He was tired of chasing her.

"Jester, I think we'll spend the night here. It'll take us all day tomorrow to get back to town. Hope you're up to it, buddy." He started to stand to gather wood.

"There's a shortcut." Her voice was hesitant and gruff as though she hadn't talked in awhile.

"I'd be obliged if you'd show it to me. I've only been in this area a few months." He went about making a fire, pretending he didn't care where she was.

"I'm doing it for the horse, mind you," she said as she stepped away from the tree.

"Of course." She was a remarkable sight. Her hair reminded him of strong, dark coffee untainted by cream as it cascaded about her shoulders. It gleamed in the afternoon sun, and her wide, brown eyes had a certain spark in them. She was a little bit of a gal, but she could pack a wallop. He fought the urge to rub his shoulder that still bore the bruise he'd gotten while rescuing her a few days ago. Once the fire was lit, he filled his coffee pot with water from the creek, and checked on Jester's foot. "You're going to be just fine. Just a bit of rest and a few days off and you'll be brand new."

He bit back a smile as she sat in front of the fire. The more he ignored her the closer she came. What a peculiar woman.

"It'll be cold tonight." ?" She shivered as she held her hands closer to the fire. "Strange isn't it how it's hot all day then it can be so cold at night? I hear they don't get much snow in Texas. Is it true?"

"Didn't bring a blanket? How about food or water?" When she shook her head, he grabbed some dried meat from his saddlebag and handed her some. "Perhaps a change of clothes? If you plan to keep running, you need to plan better. This is the last time I'm coming after you. I doubt the good folks of Asherville will turn against me if I make this my last rescue. They're getting a mite testy about not having their sheriff in town."

"I didn't know I was leaving." She shrugged her shoulders.

Shane frowned and shook his head. "Coffee?" he asked as he handed her a cup.

"Thank you. This will warm me up just fine."

He sat down and took a sip of his coffee. He stared at her until she turned beet red and turned her head. "Just how does one go about leaving without knowing about it?"

Cecily swallowed hard and gazed at him. "The night-mares come and the pain in my back… I don't know, I just start to run and I can't seem to stop." Tears shimmered in her eyes. "I know it's crazy and I'm afraid they'll put me away in a place for crazy people."

"They?"

"The whole dang town. They all watch every move I make, and they sit in judgement of me. I see it in all of their eyes. I know they want me gone from their town. Miss Edith is one of the worst. Taking me in and making herself look good to the rest of you. I liked it better at Shannon and Cinders' ranch. When Edith's not in her mercantile she's glaring at me. She puts her nose in the air and sniffs as if I'm foul. I'm not one for taking charity but for the love of God, couldn't she allow me to work in exchange for some cloth so I could make a dress? This is all I have."

"I had no idea," he said looking at her—really looking at her. Her dress was tattered and obviously had been mended in numerous places. It might have been yellow at one, time but now it was stained and honestly, it belonged in the rag bin. Her shoes needed resoling and— How had he not noticed the poor state of her clothes before now. "I bet you don't have a coat either."

"No, not anymore. When I made my trip out here to

marry that no good John Hardy I had a trunk with me. It had a few clothes and things I had in my hope chest. I'd spent years making tapestries, doilies, embroidered napkins. All kinds of things. I even had four matching tin plates. They'd cost me a lot of egg money, but I was proud I could bring them to my new husband. Never in my wildest dreams did I think I'd be handed over to an Indian and my things taken away. I've been through hell, and all people want to know is if I'm carrying. Shannon made me a dress but I lost it last time I ran." She wiped the tears from her face. "I'm sorry, none of this is your burden."

"I'm the one who's sorry. I never checked in on you after we got you back from Long Nose. He's one mean Comanche. Why did you leave Cinders' ranch? I thought you were getting along with Shannon."

"I liked everyone at Cinders' ranch, but my nightmares were keeping them up and Shannon is having a baby so I thought it best to leave."

"Well, I really thought Edith was doing right by you. She's a fickle one; likes some people and doesn't like others. I should have looked in on you. I should have made sure you had clothes to wear and shoes and a coat too."

"It's not your fault, Sheriff. You didn't know. I think the only people who really knew were the saloon girls. One of them, Noreen, asked me to come work for her. Imagine a woman owning such a place. I guess someone had to take John Hardy's place."

"Hardy won't be luring any more mail order brides out here pretending to be their fiancée."

"That's good."

"Now, what's wrong with your back?"

She shook her head. "I don't know why I even mentioned it. I'm fine."

"Did you even see the doctor?"

"I was escorted to the doctor's house by Edith and another woman named Polly. They pushed inside and demanded the doctor tell them what was done to me." The catch in her voice squeezed his heart. "They didn't ask *me* about my time with the Comanche. They asked the doctor what had been done to me. Doc Martin pushed them back out the front door and allowed me some privacy. He's a kind man."

"What did he say about your back?"

"That he'd never seen such cruelty before." Her voice drifted off as she stared into the fire.

"I'm sorry," he said wishing he had more to say.

"I'm still alive and that's something. I didn't understand much of what the Comanche said. Long Nose spoke English, but he thought it was more fun to tell me to do things in his language and beat me for failing. He spoke in English when he described what he was going to do to me." She shuddered. "I was paying for someone else's sins. John Hardy's I suspect. I know I wasn't with them for very long, but it felt like years. They ruined me and I don't know what to do or where to go. How am I supposed to fit in with other people?"

She gazed at him, her eyes full of pain, and his heart squeezed as he watched her.

"Maybe I could ask someone else to take you in. There are good people in Asherville, good families."

"Sheriff, you're one of the good guys. You can't expect everyone to see things in the same light as you. To you I'm a woman you rescued. To them I'm a heathen. I'm supposed to be full of shame and acting hysterical. I'm supposed to tell them everything that happened and I can't do it. Why do they think it's their right to know?" She gripped the fabric of her dress until her knuckles grew white. "If I told them the truth of it, they'd all most likely faint."

"What can I do to keep you from running off?"

She shook her head and shrugged her shoulders. "I really don't know. I can't stand to be cooped up or told to stay in my room all day and night. I think one day I'd like to have a place of my own where I wouldn't have to see anyone for weeks at a time."

Shane sipped his coffee and grimaced as the chilled liquid slid down his throat. "It's getting dark." He stood and grabbed his bedroll. "Here, you use this." He laid it out in front of the fire.

"What will you do?" She shook her head. "It's yours, you use it."

"Get some sleep. I'm going to sit beyond the firelight and keep watch. Long Nose might be gone, but he has friends. I'm telling you this for your own good. You were Long Nose's wife, and he treated you badly. His friends would treat you worse, I'm afraid."

Her eyes widened briefly, before she nodded. "I'm sorry, I didn't think of the danger I put you in."

Her admission surprised him. He'd thought her selfish for running away, even ungrateful but she wasn't either. She was running from her nightmares.

He stood, grabbed his rifle, and walked along the outskirts of their camp. It would be best to get a feel for the area before he found a place to keep watch. A few scattered dead twigs around the perimeter would serve as an alarm. The snapping of a twig would alert him something or someone was out there. Satisfied with his precautions, Shane found a place to sit where he wouldn't be snuck up on and waited. Three hours later, a lone wolf braved the fire and started to sneak into the campsite. Shane raised his rifle but a howl from farther away made the wolf's ears perk up and he trotted away.

The flames from the fire highlighted her thick hair. It made it look red, then lighter brown and finally it's rich deep color. It was interesting to watch and it kept him entertained most of the night. What had she'd been through? It was bound to be horrifying if she ever told him. The Comanche were fierce and brave, but they were also known for torturing their prisoners. Maybe her status as Long Nose's wife saved her from a lot of it. He wasn't about to ask, it wasn't his business. The rising sun had him back in camp, preparing coffee and gazing at Cecily's face. She had a beautiful smooth complexion and sweet red lips. Her cheekbones were high and her neck was long and graceful. She stirred in her sleep, and he hurriedly glanced away.

What parts had she left out of all she'd been through? Horrifying things, he imagined. The Comanche were fierce and brave but they were also known for torturing their prisoners. Maybe Cecily's status as a wife saved her from a lot of it. He wasn't about to ask, though. It wasn't his business.

———

THE MORNING BREEZE whispered across Cecily's face, and she panicked. Her heart quickened and she had to fight to stay still. She'd learned the hard way that lying still was her only protection from Long Nose's morning ire. He was a very big man with an extremely short temper. Keeping her eyes closed she listened to her surroundings, seeking a clue as to where he was.

Morning birdsong and other noises filtered in, and the aroma of coffee mingled with the campfire. Slowly, she remembered she was with Shane. Her muscles relaxed, and she came close to weeping. She had no cause to be afraid this morning.

The morning sun shone right into her eyes as she sat up. She blinked several times and turned her face away from the bright light and found Shane regarding her with an intense gaze. He must want to get going so he could be rid of her. Being out with her all night probably wasn't good for his reputation. Pain spiraled through her body at the admission.

Slowly she stood up trying to keep her back as straight as she could. The doctor said she'd be in pain for months to come, until the wounds healed completely. Her wounds were deep and pain would never completely disappear, but at least none had festered.

"Is it your back?" Shane asked.

She shook her head. He didn't need to know. It would only make him feel sorry for her. "It's a bit stiff is all." She stood, swallowing back a loud groan, and headed for some bushes. Before she came west, she'd have been embarrassed for a man to know what she was doing in them. Now, she was just grateful for privacy. It had never occurred to her that it was a privilege not a right. Having it taken away appalled her and something inside of her had shriveled with each indignity she'd suffered.

"Coffee?" Shane held out a battered tin cup to her when she returned.

Reaching for it, she gave him a slight smile. "Thanks. I'll drink this, and we can go." His blue eyes brightened as he nodded. He was a handsome man with wavy dark hair and very wide shoulders. He had the look of a man who worked outdoors. His shirt buttoned over a muscular chest, and she didn't see an ounce of fat on him. He was the type of man she thought she'd be marrying. Saying goodbye to her family and traveling west to marry a stranger had taken everything within. Just her luck, the stranger sold her to an Indian.

"Do you think he'll be in jail forever?"

His brow furrowed. "John Hardy? He's dead. Someone at the prison didn't take a liking to him, I suppose. Can't say I'm sorry he's gone."

"Me neither." She drank the last of her coffee took the cup

and pot, rinsed them out in the creek and put them in Shane's saddlebag. She waited for a feeling of relief now that Hardy was dead, but it didn't come. "We might as well get started. It shouldn't take too long."

They walked side by side, leading Jester behind them. "I'm surprised no one mentioned going this way to me."

"It leads to an opening in a canyon. It's the way Hardy took to deliver me to Long Nose. I tried to take note of all landscapes so I could maybe find my way home someday. I guess most people don't know it's there and go around it."

Shane nodded. "Must be the reason. Trying to remember the way home was good thinking."

She racked her brain for something interesting to say but came up blank. "Been a sheriff long?"

"I've been a sheriff in a few towns. Most of the time they stopped paying me. Lack of funds, I suppose. So far, this job has been good. The town seems to be growing, so I have a good feeling I might be able to finally put down some roots here."

"What about the war?"

"I'm from South Carolina, but I'd moved out west a few years before the war started. Had a falling out with my father over a slave, so I left. As much as I abhorred slavery, though, I couldn't condone the North telling the South what to do." He made a vague gesture with his hand. "I didn't fit on either side."

Nodding she was silent for a bit. "I'm from Pennsylvania. I grew up on a farm. It was a good life until the war. I was supposed to get married, but he died. His name was Kurt, and I'd known him all my life. His daddy had a farm next to ours and it just seemed so natural for us to fall in love." She shrugged her shoulders and kept her gaze straight ahead. "Life goes on. At least that's what my ma said."

"I'm sorry—"

"No, please don't. If you act all nice I just might cry, and I'm so afraid if I start to cry I'll never stop." She didn't dare glance at him. The silence lengthened, and she finally turned her head and gazed at him.

"I'm not sure what to say. I certainly don't want to upset you." He fiddled with Jester's reins. "I was thinking though. I might have a solution to your living arrangement. I have a house and land right at the edge of town. It's mine, I bought it outright, and I'm hardly ever there."

"I'd work for you?"

He nodded. "Sure you could cook a few meals, and you'd have a roof over your head."

She stopped walking, wrapped her arms around her middle and looked at the horizon. Her face warmed at the heat of his gaze. Making such a suggestion would have been highly improper if she'd been untouched. He wouldn't have dared to ask her into his house otherwise. But because she was tainted, moving into his house wouldn't cause a scandal, and that tore her soul. It wasn't his fault, he was only trying to give her a place to live, but still it hurt. Some things just couldn't be changed no matter how much you wished it to be with all your being. She'd never be considered respectable by anyone.

"Cecily?"

The concern in his voice was too much.

"I accept, thank you. We'd best keep going so Jester can finally rest." Without glancing at him, she continued to walk at his side wishing things were different, so very different, but she had a new lot in life, and she'd best accept it.

"I still don't see the trail through the canyon wall," he commented after a while.

"See that big oak tree? It's just to the right of it."

Shane shook his head and then squinted intently toward the area she'd pointed out. After a moment, a wide grin spread across his face. "I see it. Well I'll be. It's right near my property too."

"That's your house? The one near the canyon? It's a nice one. Somehow, I pictured a rundown shack. It's practically new." The trail through the canyon wall grew thinner, forcing them to travel single file, and she walked ahead. The light grew dim for a while but the sunshine greeted them when they were through to the other side.

"I'm glad you showed it to me. Thank you. Do you want to go into town or would you rather go to my house. I'd be glad to tell Edith you won't be back."

She didn't want to see the excitement on Edith's face when she learned she was free from her *Christian duty*. "Be sure to tell her how grateful I am for her generous hospitality."

"I sure will." They picked up their pace until they were in front of the house. "Let's get you and Jester settled. It's plenty big for both of us."

She nodded. "Yes."

"We'll each have our own room."

She nodded again. It wouldn't have mattered if it was a one room cabin. There was no way he'd touch her. "I'll try to stay out of your way."

"I need to get Jester settled in the barn. Why don't you go on in and make yourself at home."

She watched until he disappeared inside the barn before she opened the door.

The house was bigger than it looked. It had two big rooms in the front with a hallway in between them. Peeking in she noticed they were both sparsely furnished. One looked to be an office and the other a sitting room. Down the hall, the house opened up to a big room with the kitchen and another sitting room. She saw three doors at the back of the house. Behind the first was a big pantry. The shelves were a bit empty. In the middle room was a big bed and a chest of drawers in it. Shane's clothes were half hanging from the chest with some scattered on the floor. He had a lot more clothes than she. Smiling, she backed out of his room and went into the last one. This one wasn't as big as Shane's room, but contained a small bed which was all she needed. She headed back into the kitchen where the sight of the big cook stove awed her. She'd expected to cook over a fire. This house was nicer than the one she grew up in. She could be happy here, but her heart dropped. She'd only be here until Shane found himself a wife. It certainly wasn't a forever home for her. Still she'd be glad for the time she'd have. At least she hoped so.

Someone went to a lot of expense building the house. There were even glass panes in the windows. The big wooden shutters were a relief. The front door was heavy too. Perhaps she'd feel safe here.

"What do you think?"

She jumped at the sound of Shane's voice.

"It's very nice. It almost seems out of place in this town."

"That it does. It was built by the Ashers. They founded the town, but they never lived long enough to set foot into the completed house. Diphtheria is what I was told. Wiped out the whole family. I had planned to buy a big ranch with my money, but when I saw this place," he shrugged, "I don't know, I wanted it."

"I can understand why. We'll need to stock a few items so I can cook for you. We could get a few chickens and have fresh eggs."

"I was thinking maybe a cow too. The property is the perfect size for planting and the like. I haven't had much time to plan it all out. I've been busy tracking down a woman who keeps running off." He gave her a pointed look and her face heated.

"I can't make any promises. Like I said, it's them night-mares and the only thing I can do is run. I tried, really I tried hard to stay in bed, in the room, in the mercantile, but I had to get outside. I know I've caused you trouble, and I'm really sorry."

A tired grin slid over his face. "I didn't mean to make you feel bad. None of us is perfect. I need to get back to town to report you safe. I should be back for dinner. I'll have supplies delivered from Edith's place. Then my routine is to make the rounds after I eat and then again a few hours later." By the time he'd finished talking, he was at the front door. He opened it and turned back toward her. "Do you think you could check on Jester? He should be fine, but I worry." At her nod he was out the door.

The first thing she did was walk to each window and made sure they were locked. Then she looked for the root cellar hoping it was inside the house. Finally, she located it in the pantry. She pulled up on the door in the floor and went down the steps. The vastness of the room astounded her. There wasn't much food, but there were lamps, oil, candles, and blankets. Someone was stocking up in case of a siege. Too bad the original owners never got a chance to live in the house.

She was just closing the trapdoor when the jangle of a harness and the clop of hooves filtered in from outside. With a gasp, she hurried to the front windows, as her heart pounded waves of fear through her. It was Poor Boy, a young man who worked at Eats, a restaurant in town. He was rail thin with constant circles under his eyes. What was *his* reason for not sleeping?

Opening the door before he knocked, she surprised him, and his eyes widened. "I-I—Miss Edith asked me to deliver these here things to you. Well not to you exactly but to the Sheriff's house." His face turned red as he stammered.

"Can I help you unload the wagon?" She gave him what she hoped was a reassuring smile. She recognized the agony in his eyes and felt as though he was a kindred soul.

"No, Ma'am. I'm being paid for delivery."

"Okay then, you can bring the items in and put them on the table in the kitchen."

Nodding, he appeared relieved to have some direction. "Right away." He practically ran to the wagon. Perhaps his clothes had once fit, but now the shirt and pant hung loosely on his lank body. Surely Eats, the owner of the restaurant, fed him. She watched as he grabbed a box from the wagon and brought it to the house.

"The kitchen is this way."

He followed her slowly. When she turned to see what was keeping him, she noted that he took care to glance in every corner of the rooms they passed. He set the box on the table and walked back to the door, hesitated as he scanned the yard before heading back out. Such strange behavior.

Moving just as carefully, he brought in the last box and placed it next to the others. "That's all, Ma'am."

"Poor Boy, do you get enough to eat?"

"Yes, more than enough. I'm just skinny is all."

"What about sleep? You have dark circles under your eyes. Is Eats working you too hard?"

He shook his head. "No, he isn't. He's the best friend I ever had. I work hard and I get enough time to sleep. I just don't sleep much." The haunted expression on his face saddened her.

"I don't want to pry. I don't sleep much either. I have nightmares about the Comanche, and sometimes I can't stand to be in bed. That's why I ran away. I was trying to outrun my nightmares. Sometimes I'm afraid to go to bed. Is it like that for you?"

There was a flicker of awareness in his brown eyes. "Yes,

Ma'am. No one ever really understood before. I walk a lot at night."

With a nod, she gently touched his arm. "If you ever need to talk, I'm here."

"Thank you," he whispered. Then he turned and walked outside and got in the wagon without looking at her. He flicked the lines and set the horses moving. But his shoulders slouched as though he had the weight of the world on them.

What a shame, he's so young.

Shaking her head, Cecily walked into the house and locked the door. She didn't look in every corner, but she did check the windows again. They were a lot alike, Poor Boy and her, but she knew enough not to pry.

She smiled as she took the items out of the boxes. Edith had sold Shane expensive items he had no use for. He already had a skillet, Dutch oven, and a kettle. Canned peaches were a luxury he didn't need to spend his money on. Butter, bread, milk, eggs, and cheese she conceded were needed now, but she'd be able to handle making butter, bread, and cheese soon enough. The milk and eggs would come, too, as soon as they got some livestock. Store-bought soap and candles had her shaking her head again. He needed a wife to do for him. A wife who wouldn't have been taken advantage of by the shopkeeper.

She left the rest and sat down. What was she thinking? She could never be a wife, ever. Having grown up on a farm, she knew how to make most of what he'd bought, but it wasn't up to her to tell him what to do. It would serve her well to remember that before she forgot and started liking him or something. She was just the housekeeper. The excitement of unpacking the boxes dimmed. She'd mention to him that she could make a lot of what he bought. But that was it. It wasn't her home, it wasn't her household, it wasn't her money he'd just spent.

Traveling to Texas to be a bride had unnerved her. The move had been bold on her part, and she had ended up fretting the whole trip wondering if she'd made a mistake. Never in any of her ideas of what could go wrong did being given to an Indian come to mind. Even while she'd worried, she'd hoped and prayed for the best. She could go home, she supposed, but the war had decimated the farm, and her parents had told her they were relieved not to have to worry about feeding and clothing her. That was her husband's duty.

Sighing she stood and continued putting the purchases away. She would never have a husband or children. Reality was harsh and she intended to face it head on. The metallic sound of a key in the door lock sent her heart racing. She took a deep breath. Shane. It had to be Shane since he was using a key. She made her way cautiously toward the sound. Was she supposed to greet Shane or stay in the kitchen? The door swung open and Edith walked in. Surprise and dismay washed over Cecily.

"You have a key?"

"You bet your buttons I do. I've been watching over the Asher house since it was built. Nice, isn't it?" Edith walked by her and into the kitchen, leaving Cecily standing near the door with her mouth hanging open.

Cecily quickly gathered her wits and followed.

"Do you come here often? I mean since Shane bought it?"

Edith gave her a long sharp look. "You mean Sheriff O'Conner? You do work for him, right? Or was I misled about your relationship? Your reputation doesn't matter, but I am concerned about the sheriff's. His name must stand for integrity and honor, and quite frankly, I don't see him retaining those qualities with you here."

Cecily's gut tightened. "I suppose you're right."

"Or maybe the good people of Asherville will think kindly toward him for helping Cecily out," a lovely lady said as she walked into the house. "This place is nice. I wondered what it looked like inside." The blond woman moved from room to room. "I'm Addy, and you must be Cecily." She smiled. "I thought I'd get a chance to meet you at Shannon's place, but I heard you'd moved in with Edith. I have to say I'm glad you're here. Shane works so hard, he needs a hot meal when he comes home."

Cecily stared at the other woman, envying her confidence. "Please sit down. Can I get you something? Coffee or water?"

"No, thank you, though. I came to town to get a few things at the mercantile. Shane told me Edith was here. How are you, Edith?" Addy sat and sighed. "Some days I get so tired."

"I'm well enough, Addy. You really shouldn't be traveling in your condition," Edith scolded with a smile.

Addy lay her hands on her burgeoning stomach. "I know. I'm going stir crazy. Keegan has some matters to work out with the banker so Peg and I came along." She shifted her gaze to Cecily. "Peg is my little one."

Edith stared at Addy. "Did you leave her somewhere? Sometimes women in your condition aren't right in the head."

Addy laughed. "Cookie is keeping her entertained."

Edith patted her hair. "I mustn't keep Cookie waiting, or dear Peg either. Come, Addy, I'll walk you to my place."

Addy stood and winked at Cecily. "It was a pleasure meeting you."

"It was nice to meet you too." She watched them walk to the door and was shocked when Edith glanced over her shoulder and glared at her. Obviously, Edith didn't like her, but she took things too far.

Cookie was an older cowboy who worked for Cinders. What he saw in Edith she'd never know. He was the kindest, most nonjudgmental man, and Edith was his opposite. What did they find to talk about?

"Everything all right?" Shane's soft voice came from behind, and she jumped. Staring at him, words failed her, and her body began to shake.

He slowly walked to her, concern etched on his face. "I scared you, didn't I? I'm sorry," he said in a soft voice. Reaching out he cupped her shoulders in his big hands. "I want you to feel safe here. You were lost in thought." He cocked his brow and slightly tilted his head as though waiting for an answer.

"I suppose I was." She took a big step back, escaping his hands. His hands didn't scare her as much as her reaction to them. A warm tingling feeling coursed through her body. Her heart continued to beat fast, but now it wasn't out of fear. "We've had company. Poor Boy brought your purchases. Edith stopped in. Did you know she has a key and she used it to get in? Oh and I met a very nice woman, Addy. She has one child and is expecting another." She quickly glanced away.

"I'll get the key from Edith. She has no reason to let herself in. Addy Quinn is a very nice woman. Both her and her husband Keegan are pillars of the community."

"Yes, I couldn't help but notice that Edith approves of her."

"Honey, Edith is just one person. Don't let her get you down. So, did you like it?"

Frowning she wondered which item he meant. "You bought a lot of stuff. You spent more than you needed to. I can make butter and candles."

"I figured as much, but I thought we'd start off right with everything you'd need. We still need to get a cow and some chickens. I picked everything out myself." He studied her face.

What was he looking for?

"You did an excellent job. Thank you."

Shane smiled and gave her a slight nod. "I'll see you later."

"Yes, later." She went back to unpacking the boxes, waiting for Shane to leave. As soon as he did, she quickly locked the door and checked the windows yet again. She hoped she didn't end up spending her life checking windows.

One last box and it contained clothes. With great excitement, she took out the dress on the top. It was pretty blue calico with ornate buttons on it. She marveled at it. Her clothes had always been hand sewn. Under that dress lay two more. One was green while the other was bright yellow. She caressed the pretty fabric. He had gone too far. She'd have to pay him back, and she'd never be able to save any money and the box wasn't even empty. She found shoes, stockings and undergarments. On the bottom was folded cloth unlike anything she'd seen before. It looked to be sheer. Reaching in she admired the softness of the fabric as she took it out. Unfolding it, her heart dropped. It was something she imagined a whore would wear. You could see right through the material.

She refolded it and put it back in the box. He expected her to wear it to bed. How could she have been so wrong about him? He was the town sheriff. What was all that talk about his integrity? He certainly had everyone fooled. She covered her mouth as her eyes widened. Edith knew what he bought.

Back into the box went everything he had purchased for her. Her stomach burned as her eyes teared. Maybe she'd have to reconsider Noreen's offer to work at the saloon. She should see how much she'd be paid before making a decision. Glancing down at her stained, worn dress she shrugged. At least it was hers.

Cecily wandered into the front room and sat in the one

chair and stared out the window. It was time to say a final goodbye to all of her dreams. She hadn't realized she still harbored a small kernel of hope for a normal life until now. After taking a few deep breaths, she stood and put one poorly covered foot in front of the other and started for town.

CHAPTER TWO

*S*hane shook his head and looked again. Surely he didn't just see Cecily sneaking behind the buildings. He took a step and winced. Maybe next time he'd just let whoever was fighting keep on fighting. He'd just broken up a fight at the livery and had taken a hard one to his side, and it hurt like bloody hell. He walked faster trying to get to the next alley before she did, if it was Cecily. What could she be up to? Shaking his head he almost laughed. It wasn't as though he even knew her. She could be up to anything.

He waited at the end of the alley, and sure enough she went hurrying on by. This time he went down the alley to get a better look, and his mouth dropped open when she knocked on the back door to the saloon. His mouth was still gaping when the door was answered and she went inside. Of all the places in town, the saloon was the last place he would have expected her to go. What was she thinking? Perhaps she had decided to look for a job but she already had one.

He rubbed the back of his neck as he paced back and forth. Maybe waiting behind the saloon wasn't the best idea. What if she came out and saw him? She wouldn't be happy.

Cecily wasn't the type you could hem in or keep in a cage. And she certainly would not appreciate being spied on. Decision made, he rounded the corner and headed down the next alley, just far enough where he could watch the door without being seen.

He surely wished he knew what was going on in there. Maybe he should storm in and grab her. Taking off his hat, he ran his fingers through his hair wondering what the heck to do. If any of the town's women saw her, it wouldn't be good. Jamming his hat on his head, he marched back down the alley intent on saving her from herself.

As he rounded the corner, he came face-to-face with Cecily, nearly stopping his heart. Her mouth formed an O, and she had a look of guilt about her.

"What are you thinking?" he demanded. "What if one of the ladies of the town saw you in there?"

"I, well, you see Noreen offered me a job, and I wanted to see what it entailed. I had some idea of what was expected but it was more than I thought it would be. I could never willingly do that with a man, ever. I figured with what happened to me and all it would be fine, but it's not. It might seem strange to you but I still believe in virtue. My virtue was taken from me, But that doesn't mean I'll keep giving—" Her voice broke and she lowered her gaze.

He took her small hand in his and gave it a quick squeeze. "It's not your fault, none of it's your fault. Now let's get you home before the women of the town see you and turn your escapade into more fodder for gossip."

Nodding, she gave him a slight grin. "They already talk about me all the time anyway. I believe it will always be that way. I came to talk to Noreen about the job to see how much money I could make. A new town and a fresh start have been on my mind. It would be so wonderful to be someplace where no one knew me."

Shane pulled her along until they reached the front of the buildings, and then he put her arm through his and escorted her home, all the while ignoring the gawking of everyone they passed. He didn't care so much for himself, but he was outraged for Cecily. "You know, running away never solves your problems."

After they walked up the steps to his house, she let go of his arm and nodded. "Perhaps not, but I was willing to try."

"I really need to get back to town. Are you going to be all right here alone?"

She nodded hesitantly and offered a weak smile. "Did you say that you picked out everything yourself?"

"You mean the packages from the mercantile? I surely did. Hope everything is to your liking." He smiled, tipped his hat at her and walked away. Why hadn't she put on one of the new dresses he'd purchased? He'd thought that would have been the first thing she did when she saw them. Maybe they were the wrong size, or maybe she just didn't like them ... though even if she hated them, they were a far sight better than what she'd been wearing.

He shrugged his shoulders and kept walking toward town. They looked like perfectly fine dresses to him, and Edith had agreed. He'd have to ask Cecily when he got home.

HER HEART SANK as she re-examined the clothes Shane had picked out for her. It was rather impressive that he got her sizes correct even her shoes. Reaching into the box, she grabbed the sheer gown and held it up to the sunlight. It was see-through all right. What could he have been thinking? Angrily she threw the gown back into the box and gritted her teeth. She'd set him right when he got home.

It was disconcerting how gentlemanly he acted in public

compared to this purchase he'd made at the mercantile. In fact, it didn't make much sense at all. She shook her head and got busy putting away the rest of the purchases. Finally, she decided she couldn't accept any clothing at all from him, so she repacked and set the box on the floor. For the rest of the day she cooked and cleaned. She couldn't help glancing at the box and wondering what he was thinking, what he expected, and who Shane really was.

After pacing for over an hour and looking at the box, she felt more caged in than ever. She owed it to Shane to stay and talk to him about it, but she really wanted to run. Her heart sank as her hope shattered. The best thing she could do was to wait until she had enough money and move along.

The door handle jiggled, and she hurried toward it. "Who is it?" She put her ear to the door and listened.

"It's just me."

Sighing in relief, she hurriedly unlocked the door and swung it open. "You don't have a key to your own door?" He shook his head and smiled.

"I never lock the door. It looks like I need to get one made or better yet I need to get the one Edith has." He walked inside and headed straight to the kitchen. "It sure does smell good in here."

"I made fried chicken and biscuits with green beans. I hope you like it. I sure am glad you have a cook stove. I somehow imagined having to cook in the frontier over an open fire. Cinders and Shannon told me most houses don't have cookstoves." She scurried around to get the food on the table trying not to look at Shane or the box. It still bewildered her, and she wasn't quite sure how to bring the subject up. She didn't know what to say. Was she supposed to just come out and ask if he expected her to sleep with him? He sat at the table and gave her a smile as she put each item of food in front of him. His smiles weren't helping her nerves any.

He waited until she was seated before he helped himself to the chicken, biscuits and beans. She watched anxiously waiting to see if he liked it. Damn why was she so insecure? Cooking was something she excelled at and here she sat doubting herself. It made sense and didn't make sense to her all at the same time.

"This is really good, Cecily. You are an excellent cook, and I haven't had chicken like this in a very long time."

Some of the tension eased from her body but not all. There was still the box on the floor. She glanced at it periodically. When should she bring the subject up?

"Is something going on that I don't know about? You seem awfully nervous about something. If it's your cooking, you don't have to worry. I'm enjoying it, really I am." He stopped eating and stared at her as though he was waiting for an answer.

Taking a deep breath she slowly let it out. She opened her mouth then closed it and then opened it again. "I don't know what you thought our sleeping arrangements would be when you asked me to be your housekeeper."

Shane's brow furrowed as he frowned. "What are you talking about?"

Her eyes widened as she stared at him. "What am I talking about? I'm talking about the purchases you made for me of a personal nature. I was shocked when I saw them. I thought we had an understanding you'd sleep in your room I'd sleep in mine. That's what we agreed upon isn't it?"

He stared right back at her. "What are you talking about? Where did you get an idea like that? I already said you would be safe here, and I don't understand where you're getting your ideas from."

"My ideas?" She got up, fetched the box and plopped it down on the table. "What do you call these?"

"I call them clothes. Is something wrong with them? Are they the wrong sizes?"

"Oh, they are certainly the right size."

"Then what is it? You lost me somewhere, and I don't know what you're talking about. If you don't like something we can return it." Cecily stiffened at his tone of annoyance.

Putting her fists on her waist she shook her head. "Did you or did you not pick these clothes out?"

"With Edith's help." His eyes widened and a look of understanding crossed his face. "Was there something in there that was inappropriate? I did pick out the dresses and the shoes, but I left the rest up to Edith. Show me what she sent you."

After she gently took out all the dresses, the pair of shoes, stockings the undergarments she hesitated. No way she was going to dangle the see-through gown in front of him. "It's at the bottom of the box, help yourself." She quickly turned her back on him as her face heated.

"Well, now I see what got your feathers ruffled. I did not pick this out. I wouldn't do anything to embarrass you. You've been through enough." His voice softened. "Don't worry about it I'll have a little chat with Edith. She has no right trying to make our arrangement seem sinful. I can't change what happened to you, and I'm sorry about that, but I would never disrespect you."

Her relief was so great, tears trailed down her face, and she dashed them away quickly with her hands. He was the man of honor she had thought he was, and a bit of her faith in people was restored. "Thank you for that. My mind has been whirling with all sorts of thoughts since I saw that— that *thing* in the box." She wrapped her arms around her middle trying to keep herself from falling apart. It wouldn't do for him to think she was even more crazy than she already was.

"Leave it to Edith to try to cause trouble. I really don't understand that woman. She's nice as pie to some and is mean as a rattler to others. I'm sorry she has you in her sights, it's just plain unfair. But I want you to know that not all people are like Edith. In fact, most people out west mind their own business." Shane got up and walked until he stood right in front of her. He grabbed her hand and rubbed the back of it with his work worn thumb. "Darlin', I'm not saying things won't be rocky for a while, but I believe people will come to accept you just as I have."

Cecily gazed into his compassion-filled eyes and wished she could just walk into the circle of his arms. He gave her comfort, made her believe in herself, and his arms around her sure would be wonderful. She mentally shook herself. Better not to wish for things that would never, ever happen. She worked for Shane; that was all, and it would be best for her to keep her distance.

"Well, I'm glad that we have that settled." Relief rushed through her, and it made breathing easier. "I have to admit it had me shaken most of the day, and I wasn't sure how to approach you about it. Thank you for making it easy to talk to you. Most men aren't like that." She began gathering the dirty dishes. "I'd best get the dishes done. It's been a long day, and I have to admit I'm tired."

"Here, let me help you. Many hands make light work, my mama used to say and truthfully I'm tired too." He gave her an easy grin, and she nodded.

"It's not necessary, but just this once it would be nice thank you."

She washed and he dried, making the cleanup much faster and easier. Afterwards, she said goodnight and went into her own room with her new clothes in her arms. She shut the door and leaned against it, closing her eyes as she took a deep breath. Things might just work out after all. Damn that Edith! That woman was a back stabber for sure, and Cecily would be well served to remember it.

———————

SHANE RAN his fingers through his hair. What the heck had just happened? He knew Edith could be mean but this was beyond mean. No wonder Cecily had gone to the saloon looking for a job. She probably figured if sleeping with him was a requirement she might as well check out her options. He didn't blame her one bit. In fact, it took a lot of courage to go to the saloon. He didn't know many women that would do that.

Cecily was one-of-a-kind. She had great strength about her. She also had kindness, and she seemed damn smart. Tomorrow he'd see about getting that cow and some chickens and whatever else was needed to make his place into a farm. Not a big farm—he didn't have time for that— but one big enough to make Cecily happy. He would've expected her to cower and hide in the corner of each room but instead she'd exhibited gumption.

He smiled as he thought about her concern for his money. She had made sure he knew that she could make almost everything he'd purchased. What was a damn shame she got mixed up with John Hardy and Long Nose; she would've made a great frontier wife. Stretching his arms above his head, he yawned. He still had one more round to make. He grabbed his gun belt, a jacket, and his hat and out the door he went.

He smiled as he heard the lock clicked as soon as he closed the door. He'd better get the key back from Edith. If Cecily fell asleep he'd have no way of getting back into the house. He shook his head. It wouldn't be the first time he'd spend the night at the jailhouse.

Walking for a bit he finally made it into town and onto the boardwalk. The first place he checked was the saloon. It usually got rowdy in there at night, especially on the weekends and from the sound of it, tonight was no exception. Clinking glasses, loud voices, and off-tune piano music greeted him as he stepped through the swinging doors. He quickly scanned the room keeping his eyes open for any sign of trouble. The usual crowd of cowboys all drinking and carousing. A poker game was going on at the table near the corner of the bar. He was familiar with two of the players but the other two he'd never seen before.

After nodding to Jamie, the bartender, he moseyed over to the table in the corner. He didn't get too close; he wanted to be able to observe all four of them at the same time. He leaned against the wall and folded his arms in front of him keeping his gaze on them at all times. From his experience, new faces playing poker usually meant trouble, and this one promised no different. He inwardly groaned, the two men he did know were both cowboys. Cyrus was unmarried, but he was not a rich man. Bill was married with three little ones. Shane sighed, neither of these men could afford to lose. The other two men were well-dressed, and he'd bet his next meal, were professional gamblers. This was the first time he'd ever seen professionals in Asherville, and it didn't sit well with him. He had a bad feeling in his gut that it was not going to end well.

Giving up all hope of a quiet evening, he pushed himself away from the wall and walked closer to the table. "Howdy, gentlemen, seems like a lively game you've got going on. Bill, Cyrus, good to see you," he said as he nodded to them.

They both looked up, nodded back and quickly went back

to the game, and Shane suppressed a groan. Seemed like they were already in deep.

He turned to the newcomers. "I haven't seen you two around before. I'm Sheriff O'Connor, and you are…?"

The dark-haired man leaned back, took a gulp of his whiskey, and stared at Shane. His hair was slicked against his head, and his jacket and vest were obviously tailor-made. "Diamond is my name, Fred Diamond. Nice to meet you, Sheriff," the man said in a southern drawl.

The other man was dressed in much the same manner. His hair was blond, his eyes beady, and fancy clothes. An expensive gold chain looped from the watch pocket of his shiny red and black vest, likely connected to an equally expensive watch. "It's a pleasure, Sheriff O'Connor."

"And your name is?"

"Thomas McIntyre."

"You fellas aren't from around here, are you?"

"Diamond and I hail from Georgia. We heard of your lovely town and just had to stop." Thomas McIntyre quickly looked away and studied his cards.

Shane smiled. "Well as long as you keep the game friendly—"

"Don't you worry none, Sheriff," Fred Diamond said as he gave a fake smile.

Shane narrowed his eyes and stared the gambler down. "Just make sure you do keep it friendly, gentlemen. We don't cotton to any trouble around here." Shane walked back toward the bar and nodded to Jamie. "I don't trust those two. If you need me I'll be spending the night at the jail just in case."

Jamie nodded as Noreen sauntered over smiling at Shane. "Have you come to enjoy my fine establishment?"

"As fine as it is, Noreen, I'm afraid I'm going to have to

pass. I just told Jamie I'll be at the jailhouse all night in case I'm needed. I have a feeling there's going to be trouble."

She leaned toward him until her breasts almost fell out of her dress. "You may be right, Sheriff, but I'm hoping it's nothing I can't handle." She winked at him.

"Well you know where I'll be." With a tip of his hat at Noreen, Shane walked out of the saloon. He headed back to the jail, grabbed his rifle and made sure it was loaded. Next, he put on a pot of coffee. It was going to be a long night.

THE NEXT MORNING when Cecily awoke she wasn't sure where she was. When she remembered she was safe in Shane's house, she smiled. It was the first time in a long time she felt safe. Usually she was up before the sun; she could only hope she hadn't missed making breakfast for Shane. Quickly, she pulled on her new green dress. The fresh fabric caressed her legs and ankles as she twirled, enjoying the glorious feeling of owning something new. Shane certainly was a very generous man, and she was a lucky girl even if it was for only little while.

She opened the door and walked into the kitchen, unnerved by the deep quiet. Shane's gun belt and hat were gone, so she must've missed him this morning. Damn, her first day on the job and already she'd messed it up. Perhaps bringing him lunch would make up for his lack of breakfast. She sat down on the chair trying to make up her mind as to whether going into town was a good idea or not. Certainly, she'd rather not, but she owed it to Shane. There was plenty of leftover fried chicken, and she'd make him fresh biscuits.

Having a plan of action, a purpose, made her feel better. She put the coffee on, grabbed the broom and went about cleaning the house. As she swept the pantry, she noticed the door to the root cellar was too obvious. It wouldn't make a good place to hide unless she could find a way to cover it. Maybe she could make a rag rug to cover it. Her old dress was certainly a rag, and she'd see what she could find around the house.

She checked the windows one by one inwardly groaning at her compulsion. Then she checked the front door. The knob didn't move. She caught her breath. Locked! And Shane had no key. Oh, no. He'd been locked out all night. Dismay filled her. How could she have done such a thing? Hurriedly, she made the biscuits, put the food in the basket and raced out the door, intent on making amends. Dismay washed over her as she realized clouds had blotted out the sun, and a light drizzle had started to fall. She'd have to hurry so her new dress wouldn't get wet and muddy.

Her pace was fast until she got to town then a combination of dread and the hope of being invisible slowed it to a crawl.. Thank goodness the sheriff's office wasn't too far inside town limits. Her only hurdle was the mercantile, which was situated across the street from the jail. Once the jail was in sight, she increased her pace hoping to get there without running into Edith, but her hopes were dashed as Edith came out of the mercantile and quickly crossed the street.

"Yoo-hoo, Cecily, wait for me." Cecily bit her lip and waited. "Poor Shane spent the night in the jail. Did you do something to make him unwelcome in his own home?"

"That's none of your business."

"Why, you ungrateful little wretch. A man gives you a place to stay and you lock him out?"

Cecily seethed inside but she was not going to give Edith the satisfaction of knowing she'd made her mad, so she forced a smile. "Well, I'll be on my way to see Shane. Good day to you, Edith." Then she turned and walked away. She could feel the heat of Edith's stare on her back. Did the whole town know that Shane was locked out last night? She stood in front of the jailhouse and hesitated. What if he fired her? Her hand shook as she opened the door.

Shane sat leaning back in his chair with his feet on his desk, sleeping. Loud snores echoed in the sparsely furnished room, and Cecily smiled. Whether a man snored or not was such a personal thing to know. Should she wake him up or let him sleep? She decided to let him sleep. As quietly as possible she left the basket of food on the corner of the desk and snuck back out. To her dismay, Edith was standing there waiting for her.

"You'll be leaving on the next stage?" Edith asked in a sarcastic voice while looking Cecily up and down.

Cecily's eyes widened and her first instinct was to walk away from Edith. "Of course not. In fact, we need to get the key from you now. Do you have it on you or would you like me to accompany you to the mercantile so you can get it?" Cecily asked in a smug voice.

Edith's mouth dropped open. "Well we'll just see about that."

"Go right ahead," Cecily said with the confidence she did feel. "But I have to warn you, Shane said he was going to take a nap, and he didn't want to be disturbed."

Edith's eyes narrowed as she stared at Cecily long and hard. Finally, she shrugged her shoulders, reached into her pocket and withdrew a key. She slapped it into Cecily's hand. "I'd watch your step if I were you. I'm glad I had the key on me since you are not welcome in the mercantile. I refuse to have your kind in my store."

Cecily turned, clutching the key in her hand, and proceeded home. The light rain grew heavier, chilling her already shaking body.

"Damn that Edith," she muttered. She'd just have to learn

to ignore her. She had a feeling it wasn't going to be easy. Edith seemed to be everywhere. A loud boom of thunder startled her. She hastened her walk until she got to the edge of town and then she ran. Until she'd come west, thunderstorms were about the only thing that had ever scared her. It began to pour, but luckily, she wasn't far from the cabin. Her footsteps clopped heavily on the board porch as she raced for the door and flung it open. Quickly, she closed and locked it behind her, wet fingers slipping at first on the latch

She was frozen to the core, but she needed to make sure the house was secure. Dripping water as she went from room to room, she checked the windows to be sure they were locked. Shivers raced over her as she built up the fire in the stove until the wood crackled as it burned. Only then did she decide she was safe enough to change her clothes. Quickly she went into her room, she grabbed a towel and undressed. Once again, she admired the fine quality of the clothes. She rubbed the chemise against her skin astounded that anything could be so soft.

She wished she had a full-length mirror, she wanted to see what she looked like in her new dress and shoes. Her old things hung from a peg in the wall, and she was so tempted to burn them, but using them for her braided rug seemed more prudent. Waste not want not; she'd heard that all her life, and they were words that had served her well. With a sigh, she bent over and lifted the wet green dress then carried it into the kitchen where she draped it over a chair to dry.

A smile lingered on her face as she touched the collar, the sleeves, and the full skirt of the blue dress. This could've been her happiness yesterday if not for Edith. Oh, that woman was a snake in the grass, one that was just waiting for the right time to strike out. Edith had enough venom inside her to create a lot of problems. Cecily would have to watch her back.

A tremendous boom shook the house, and she screamed. Somehow the storms seem worse in Texas than they had in Pennsylvania. Maybe it was all the open country and the fact that you could see for miles and miles. Everything inside her demanded she go and check the windows again, but she refused. Her hand shook as worry filled her body. She needed to keep busy.

Grabbing the Dutch oven she decided to make a treat as a thank you to Shane for buying her the clothes. The provisions Shane had bought from the mercantile had included several jars of canned fruit, including some peaches. She had made many a fine peach cobbler back in Pennsylvania. In fact, she'd won many ribbons at the town fairs where she grew up. She grabbed the ingredients she needed and in no time she had her peach cobbler ready to go. The aroma reminded her of happier times on the farm with her family before the War Between the States. There'd been so much to look forward to: a home of her own with a husband and children. She'd thought she'd live next to her parents and they would share their joys together. Instead, they shared the loss of loved ones and the loss of their dreams.

The rain was making her feel melancholy. It was raining the day she'd learned that her fiancé was dead. And the day she'd learned her brother was dead. She'd never given the rain much thought until now. She'd always been a dreamer and a planner, and now she wasn't able to do either. In fact, she didn't know what she was anymore. To most people she was damaged beyond repair and no longer human.

She shook her head. She'd spent a good amount of time helping those less fortunate than she. Her father often scolded that she would give away the farm if someone needed it. Why couldn't people just treat each other with respect and kindness? She didn't understand how being mean to others could make one feel better inside unless all they had to give was pure meanness.

Finally, she couldn't stand it anymore. She'd done everything she could to keep herself from checking the windows but it was a compulsion she just couldn't stop. She shook her head as she went from room to room making sure the house was secure. She lingered at the front window wondering when Shane would be back. Probably not until dark, she mused as she turned and went back into the kitchen. At least she was warm and had a roof over her head and new clothes to wear, things could be a lot worse.

After putting the cobbler in the oven, she grabbed her old clothes and a pair of scissors and went about starting her braided rug. Strange how different things were out here. At home open windows and open doors were the normal state of things. Would she ever get to a point where she'd be able to live that way again?

CHAPTER THREE

Shane awoke at his desk pleasantly surprised to see the basket of food waiting for him. Edith sure did spoil him something awful. He swung his feet off the desk and eagerly sat up diving into the basket of food. A big smile crossed his face when he realized the food was from Cecily and not Edith. The food looked good, and he enjoyed each and every bite.

The door flew open, revealing Poor Boy just outside. His eyes were wide and his breathing heavy. "Sheriff you gotta come! There's trouble at the saloon. It's them gamblers. You'll need your gun or two. In fact, you might want to bring a couple shotguns too."

"What in tarnation?" Shane jumped up, made sure his gun was loaded, filled his pockets with extra bullets, and grabbed his shotgun. He jammed his hat onto his head and flew out the door past Poor Boy. He'd known those two men were trouble the moment he'd set eyes on them. Gamblers didn't belong in a small town like Asherville. He ran down the boardwalk, feet clomping heavily, and crossed the street.

Flattening his back against the front of the saloon, he peered into the window.

The man who'd introduced himself as Fred Diamond had his gun drawn, and he was using Noreen as a shield. Shane scanned the room for his partner McIntyre and spotted him still sitting at the poker table as though nothing was happening. He finally saw Old Will standing with his gun pointed at Diamond. Damn they must've fleeced Old Will, and that farmer was dirt poor. He had no business in a poker game. Where did he get the money to stake himself?

Shane entered the saloon, gun in hand and stared at Fred Diamond. He portrayed a calmness he did not feel. "What's the problem? Let Noreen go. If this is between you and Old Will it's cowardly to hide behind a woman."

Fred Diamond gave Shane a pointed look. "This old coot is trying to kill me for no good reason. I'm just trying to keep that from happening."

Shane shook his head, "Now what's this all about, Old Will?"

Old Will's gun shook in his hand as he spoke. "Them there cheaters stole my money. Stole every penny, every last one. Cheating is what they're doin', and I aim to put a stop to it. Now, Shane, I asked politely for my money back but they don't speak politeness. So if I gotta put a few holes in one or both of them that's just what I'm gonna do."

Shane kept his eye on McIntyre, not trusting him one bit. In fact, he didn't look concerned at all. "Well, Diamond, just give Old Will his money back. He's not a rich man." Shane glanced at Old Will and frowned. "What were you thinking getting involved in a poker game?"

"To my utter shame, I thought I could make a fast buck. I heard around town about people winning, and I figured I could use the money. Oh, they're good all right, they ease you in and let you win, and just when they think you're about to leave the table, they start winning, and the next thing you know you're piss poor. Well I'm not taking it from them. I might be foolish, but I ain't stupid. Now I want my money back or things are going to get ugly."

Noreen's eyes shimmered with tears. "Shane, you've got to help me. I don't want to die."

"The first thing we're going to do is get everyone out of the saloon including Noreen. She's not part of your disagreement. Let her go." A few stragglers left the bar.

Diamond pushed Noreen in Old Will's direction. She stumbled across the dusty floor and fell into him, knocking his gun from his hand. Diamond whirled and aimed his gun at Shane and pulled the trigger, but Shane raised his first. Diamond opened his mouth in surprise and staggered sideways. Something struck Shane in the shoulder and searing agony tore through him. Gritting his teeth, he turned and shot McIntyre dead.

His chest squeezed against the pain, and he dropped to his knees on the hard saloon floor. Breathless, he glanced up at Old Will. "Go...get your money."

IT WAS GETTING LATE, and the sun had set hours before. Cecily rubbed the back of her neck trying not to worry about Shane. For all she knew this was a normal occurrence. Of course he didn't have typical work hours. He was probably just late. At least the rain had finally stopped along with the booming thunder. She'd eaten about an hour ago, and she had to admit the cobbler was one of her best.

She got as far as she could with the braided rug, she needed more rags. She'd have to ask Shane about that. Too bad there weren't any books to read. A sense of loneliness enveloped her, but at least she didn't feel hemmed in. She didn't feel the need to run. Shrugging her shoulders, she admitted that was a good thing.

She stood to put more wood on the fire when a knock on the door interrupted her. She quickly made her way to the front door and hesitated before opening it. It took courage but she turned the knob and pulled.

Two men stood outside, Shane leaning heavily between them. With a gasp, Cecily stepped out of the doorway so they could carry him inside.

"This way." She rushed to his bedroom, aware of them following her, and quickly pulled the quilt off the bed to make it easier to place Shane on it. She watched in horror as men she didn't know carefully set him down. When the doctor appeared in the doorway, she calmed a bit. "What happened? Is it serious? Is he gonna die?"

Dr. Martin thanked the men and shooed them on their way. "It's just a shoulder wound. It's really not all that serious, nothing he hasn't had before."

Her heart beat painfully against her rib cage as she rubbed her hands. "How did this happen? Was he shot?"

Edith stepped inside and maneuvered herself between the doctor and Cecily. "Don't you worry none, doc, I'll make sure Shane is cared for. You go on home and tell that sweet wife of yours I said hello."

Dr. Martin glanced from one woman to the other with a worried look on his face. "Edith, I'm sure Cecily here can take care of Shane. After all you have the mercantile to run. Unless of course Cecily can take your place at the store."

Edith's eyes opened wide in horror. "I would never allow such a thing to happen. Why I'd lose all my business. Perhaps you're right, Dr. Martin. Like you said, this isn't Shane's first bullet wound." She turned and narrowed her eyes as she stared at Cecily. "You'd best take good care of the sheriff. I'll be back in the morning to check up on you."

Cecily swallowed her words of anger and turned her back on Edith. "Dr. Martin, what do I need to do in order to take care of Shane?"

"He's more than likely to burn up with fever. Washing him with cool water usually helps. I'll be by in the morning to change his bandage. Oh, he'll probably be restless, and I need you to keep him as still as possible. He'll be fine my dear. I'll see you in the morning."

Dr. Martin started for the door and then turned around. "Come along, Edith, I'll walk you home."

Cecily barely heard the door close she was so intent on Shane. She hurried to the kitchen and splashed cool water into a large bowl, then grabbed a cloth from one of the drawers. She also lugged in a kitchen chair and set it all beside the bed. Her heart squeezed as she gazed at him. Reaching down she tenderly brushed the hair off his forehead.

His eyes popped open and he pinned her in a pained gaze.

"You're awake," she exclaimed in surprise, quickly removing her hand from his forehead.

"I've been awake. Edith kept demanding that they take me to her place. She seems to think she's the only one who can take care of me. I gave Dr. Martin my final instruction to bring me home, and I closed my eyes. I didn't feel up to arguing with that woman. I'm glad she finally left." He grimaced as he turned his head toward Cecily.

"You're in pain. What can I do to help you? The doctor didn't leave me anything to give to you." She rubbed her hands helplessly.

"He already gave me something for the pain. It's not so bad now that I'm home. At least I can relax here and know that you're not the type of woman to fuss over a man."

Cecily smiled at him, but on the inside she wondered why he thought that of her. She'd taken care of various family members when they had been sick, and yes she had fussed over them. Did she seem so changed now?

Leaning over she put her hand on his cheek to gauge whether or not he had a fever. So far so good, he was still cool to the touch. "Do you need anything or should I let you get some sleep?" She straightened up and glanced away, his comments about her not fussing bothered her.

"I could use some shuteye. Make sure the door is locked and get some rest for now. If I end up with a fever you won't be getting much sleep I'm afraid, that is unless you let Edith into the house." He gave her a weary smile and then closed his eyes.

She stared at him for a while, wondering what had happened. The answers would have to wait until tomorrow. Rushing to the front door she turned the lock and was satisfied when she heard a click. She started back toward the kitchen, pausing yet again to check the windows. After wandering back into Shane's room, she stared at herself in a small piece of mirror he probably used for shaving. She looked the same as she always had, but somehow people thought she was different. She *was* different, but how could they tell by just looking at her? How did he know whether she was the fussy type or not? She would fuss over him if she wanted to. She put her hands over her heated cheeks and turned away from the mirror. She couldn't help what others thought. What they perceived and what she really was, were two entirely different things, and she didn't know why Shane's words affected her so.

She needed to get some sleep because if he ended up with a fever, she'd be awake for some time to come. She took off her blue dress berating herself for thinking herself pretty while she was wearing it. It didn't matter what she wore, she'd always be the woman who'd been kidnapped by the

Indians. Finally, she crawled into bed and promptly fell asleep.

She thought she was dreaming but when she finally forced her eyes open, she heard Shane groaning. Quickly, she pushed her covers off and leaped out of bed, hurried into the kitchen, lit the oil lamp and headed into Shane's room. There was no need to touch him to know he had a fever. Sweat poured off his body and his face was tinged red. His eyes were still closed as he thrashed around groaning. Thankful for the supplies she'd left in his room, she quickly wet a cloth and began to wipe down his face. She was going to have to get his shirt off. Why on earth had they put it back on him? Shaking her head, she began to unbutton the bloody shirt, slowly exposing his hard muscled chest.

She wanted to take the shirt completely off but wasn't sure if it would jostle his wound so she decided to leave it on for now. Carefully, she washed his chest and stomach avoiding his wound. He was all-male and the sight of him made her mouth dry. Heat radiated off him, and she was worried. The house was cold, and he was so hot. What if she did something wrong and he died? She shook her head, she couldn't think that way. She was doing the best she knew how.

She went to the stove, added more wood, and put on some coffee to boil. She didn't know what time it was. It was still very dark outside but she decided this might be her only chance to get a few things done, she went into her room, got dressed then walked out of her room re-braiding her hair. She stuck her head into Shane's room to see how he was faring. His groaning had quieted for the moment, and she sighed in relief. Some food would probably be good for him when he woke up. Gathering all the ingredients she needed she put together a simple broth, placed it in a pot and put it on the stove. Finally, she poured herself a cup of coffee then went back into Shane's room. She sat beside him continually bathing his head and chest with cool water.

He was such a handsome man, a kind man, a man of integrity, and she'd never known another like him. He'd been good to her, and she planned to fuss over him like no one had ever fussed before, despite his assertion that he didn't want that. Of course, Edith's fussing was probably some form of torture.

When his face relaxed, he looked so young and carefree, and she bet he had been that way as a child. Her back began to ache from leaning over him, so she stood, stretching her arms over her head. She walked to the front door, checked that it was locked and then made herself walk past the windows with only a glance. Progress.

IT FELT like a red-hot branding iron was in his shoulder and he could barely move his arm. Shane opened his eyes and looked around, relieved to be in his bedroom but bewildered as to why. Then it came back to him; the saloon, the gamblers, and Old Will. He groaned, not so much due to the pain as to the amount of time he'd be laid up. At least he wasn't in a room above the mercantile.

Cecily walked in looking pretty as a picture in her new blue dress. She had a mug of coffee in one hand and what looked to be a bowl of water in the other. She placed the items down on the table next to his bed and took a seat. He smiled as he waited for her to look at him. She jumped when she realized he was awake and he almost laughed. "Have I been out long?"

"Not really just long enough for a good night's sleep. You have a nasty fever, though." She gave him a worried smile.

"I feel a mite hot." He still had his shirt on and wanted to laugh. "You do know the best way to get a fever down is to bathe the patient with cool water."

"Yes, in fact I do know that, and I've been doing that very thing for hours."

"But my shirt is still on."

"Of course it is, but it's unbuttoned. They brought you to me with your shirt on, and I didn't want to take a chance of opening your wound by pulling it off. Plus I wasn't sure if it was proper." She turned her head away but not before he saw the bloom of redness in her cheeks.

"Well, I'm awake now so why don't we get the shirt off? Here, help me sit up." He waited until she was beside him before he moved. Her hands felt good on his back. Taking his uninjured arm out of the sleeve was easy. As she walked to the other side of the bed to help with the other sleeve there was a knock on the door.

Heaving a sigh, she gave him a smile and left to go answer.

Attempts to get the sleeve off himself became too painful. Besides, it'd be more fun to have Cecily's help. Listening hard, he tried to distinguish who was at the door. He heard Dr. Martin's voice, then Edith's voice, and he smiled when he recognized Shannon's voice. He watched as they trooped inside, one by one, with Cecily trailing far behind. Somehow her being at the end of the line didn't seem right.

"What are you trying to do? Why are you taking off your shirt?" Edith arched her eyebrow as she stared at Cecily then she hurried to his side and tried to put his shirt back on him.

"Ouch, Edith, you're hurting me. Let go," he said.

Dr. Martin put his hand on Shane's forehead and nodded. "You've got a fever all right. Nothing to worry about though. You'll pull through." He retrieved a bottle out of his bag and handed it to Cecily. "This is laudanum for his pain I'll write the instructions down for you before I leave."

Cecily reached for the bottle and held it to her chest, nodding. "I'd appreciate that."

Shannon smiled at him. "You had us worried, my friend. We got word you were shot but no details." She walked to his left side and helped him take the rest of his shirt off. "Here, this will make it easier for Cecily to keep you cool." She held her hand up in Edith's direction. "I don't want to hear it, so just save your judgments for yourself."

Edith gasped and sputtered then she snatched the shirt from Shannon. She grabbed a clean shirt off the wall peg and marched around the bed to Shane's right side and tried to catch his arm so she could put it in the sleeve.

"Oh, for heaven sake, leave Shane alone. Dr. Martin, what do you think? Shirt on or shirt off?" Cecily asked as she thumped the laudanum down on the bed side table.

"Off. If he gets hot enough she'll have to bathe his back too." He gazed at Edith and shrugged his shoulders. "Sometimes it's not about what's proper, it's about caring for the patient. The important goal here is to make Shane well again." Dr. Martin glared at Edith then gave Shane a much friendlier look. "Now, Shane, I didn't have a chance to ask you how you feel."

"Truthfully I feel a mite better now that my shirt is off." He sighed. "Thanks for coming to my rescue, doc. I'm sure Cecily can handle it. I have complete faith in her."

"Good, good I can see you are in capable hands so I will be back later this afternoon to check on you." He closed his bag, shook Shane's hand and nodded to the women before he left.

Shannon moved closer to the bed. "I'm glad it's not too serious. I'm also glad you have Cecily here to take care of you. Do you need anything? Cecily, I could cook up a few meals or do laundry, whatever you need."

Cecily smiled. "You are a dear, sweet woman, Shannon,

and I appreciate your offer, but I think for now Shane just needs rest."

Shannon took Cecily's hand giving it a quick squeeze then leaned down and kissed Shane on the cheek. "You get better now you hear?"

Shane nodded.

Shannon looked at Edith. "We'd best get going don't you think?"

Edith put her hands on her hips and shook her head. "In my day we'd never even think of seeing a man without a shirt on. You two women are two of a kind. Neither of you have any respect for propriety. I feel sorry for you both. You'll never have the respect of the right people."

Shannon laughed. "Fine by me. We'll be going, now." She pulled a protesting Edith toward the bedroom door. "Take care, Shane, and it was nice to see you, Cecily," she called over her shoulder.

Shane laughed and shook his head his smile dimmed as his gaze met Cecily's unhappy one. "Don't let Edith ruin your day. She is in no way a reflection of how the rest of the town thinks. I've always thought of her as a mere nuisance, but I can see she's hurting you. I'll talk to her—"

"No please don't. It'll only make things worse, and I'm fine actually really I am." She picked up the cloth, wet it again, and carefully wrung it out before placing it on Shane's forehead. The cloth felt like heaven on his hot face.

He moaned in pleasure and closed his eyes, waiting for her to continue, but when she didn't, he opened his eyes again. She sat in her chair with her hand in midair staring at his chest. There was no way to tell from her expression what she was thinking. Did she think him ugly with his many scars? Or was it something else? Something deeper? After all she'd been through, a man's chest probably scared her.

"You don't have to do this, you know. The sight of a near

naked man must bring back bad memories. I know they're memories best forgotten, if possible. Give me the cloth I can wipe down my own chest."

Her gaze met his and she almost laughed. "Wipe down your own chest? You are amusing when you want to be," she said as she shook her head.

"I'm not trying to be funny I'm just trying to make things easier for you."

Squirming in her chair she sighed. "Your chest is nothing like Long Nose's chest. His was a darker color and hairless. You both have well-muscled chests, but yours has a sprinkling of dark hair across it. And of course with your fever and gunshot wound, I don't find you particularly threatening."

He wanted to tell her how pretty she looked in her dress, but he knew his opinion wouldn't be welcome. "You've been getting enough rest, haven't you?"

She stood and stretched her back by arching backwards. "It's only been a day, not even a whole day and yes I got enough rest. Don't worry about me just worry about getting yourself well. I'm going to get fresh water and a cup coffee. Would you like a cup?"

"Water will do for now, thank you." He watched her leave his room. Somehow she took all the sunshine and happiness along with her.

CECILY FANNED her face with a piece of paper. If only he knew. She smiled at his concern for her. She didn't feel in the least bit threatened. In fact, he fascinated her a bit too much. Many times when she'd stroked the cloth over him she'd been tempted to touch him with her bare hands. What a hussy she was. She began to laugh but her humor died as she thought of Edith. That woman had become the bane of her existence, and she couldn't allow it. She'd have to try her best to not take Edith's cruel words and actions to heart.

The world was full of crosses to bear, and she'd had more than her share, but she'd get through it. Right now her main concern was Shane. She still hadn't found out how he had been shot. She'd just finished pouring herself a cup of coffee when another knock on the door startled her. After she caught her breath, her shoulders sagged. Now what?

She cracked open the door and smiled when she recognized Poor Boy, who stood hat in hand on the front porch. She opened the door wider. "Come on in, Poor Boy."

He took a step back and shook his head. "Miss. Cecily, I'm here to ask a favor. Now don't feel you have to say yes or anything like that. I knows it's hard for people to get by these days and all but Eats' restaurant just done burn down."

Cecily clapped a hand to her chest. "Did anyone get hurt in the fire?"

"No, no one. Eats was out, and I was asleep on the kitchen floor but I got out."

"What are you going to do now?" Her eyes widened in understanding. "Do you need a place to stay? What about Eats? Where is he staying?"

Poor Boy's face turned beet red. "Eats him got himself a woman, and there's no room for me." He stared at the wooden porch floor, shifting his weight from one leg to the other. "You probably know this already, but most people don't take to me, but you and Sheriff O'Connor have always shown me kindness. You have a nice barn and only one horse. I was thinking, I was asking, can I sleep in your barn? I can hunt for food, and I know how to take care of myself. I know the sheriff got himself all shot up, and maybe I could help." He peeked up at her and then quickly looked down at the floor again. "You know, now that I thunk it all out, I'll be going." He turned to walk away.

"Poor Boy, hold up a minute."

He stopped and faced her.

She tilted her head and studied him. What was his real story? Not that it was any of her business. "There's no room in the barn, but we have plenty of room in the house. Come on in." She opened the door wider and gestured with her hand for him to enter.

Poor Boy hesitated then he stepped inside. "I don't want to make more work for you or be of no trouble."

"Come on let's get you into the kitchen and warmed up and don't worry, you won't be any trouble. In fact, you can help me take care of the sheriff."

Poor Boy's smile beamed. "I'd be awfully proud to help out the sheriff."

"What's going on out there?" The sheriff yelled.

Eyes wide, Poor Boy jumped. His breaths came short and quick, and he looked as though he wanted to run. "Come on, Poor Boy, let's go talk to the Sheriff." Cecily led the way into Shane's room as Poor Boy shuffled right behind her. She glanced over her shoulder as they entered the room, and Poor Boy quickly lowered his head.

"Good to see you, Poor Boy," Shane said as he flashed a questioning gaze at her.

She waited for Poor Boy to speak, but he didn't. "Eats burned down and Poor Boy needs a place to stay. I told him it was fine, but since it's your house, I suppose we should ask you."

"Poor Boy, you are more than welcome to stay as long as you need. Now tell me, was anyone hurt?" Shane started to push himself up into a sitting position and she was right there pushing him back down on the bed. He gave her a look of annoyance then stayed put.

"No sir, no one was hurt. Eats, he was with his lady friend, and I was asleep on the kitchen floor. I smelled smoke and saw it wasn't coming from the kitchen so I got up. The front of the building was on fire. I lit out the back way and got Eats. I never seen Eats cry before, and I've been with him a long time."

"Did you see who set the fire?"

"No, sheriff, I ain't seen nothing. Eats told me to find a place to stay until he had time and the gumption to rebuild. I thought I could stay in your barn for a while, but Miss Cecily invited me in the house. I'll go if you want." Poor Boy finally looked Shane in the eye as he bit his lip and swallowed hard.

"Of course you're welcome to stay in the house. We'll get it all figured out once I'm on my feet. I could probably help Eats rebuild."

Poor Boy grinned from ear to ear. His clothes were tattered and torn and covered in dirt. On top of the dirt was a layer of soot that covered him from head to toe.

Cecily stared at him wondering just how old he really was. "Well, good I'm glad that's settled," Cecily said. "I do think the first thing we need to do is get you washed up and into some clean clothes."

Poor Boy grimaced and shook his head. "Ma'am my own clothes is just fine. I don't want to be a bother, and I'll not take charity from no one."

She admired Poor Boy's pride. "It's not charity I'm offering. In fact, there's a lot of work that needs to be done around here. Isn't that right, Shane? Why we need to get the farm started and that takes a lot of work."

Poor Boy nodded. "I lived on a farm once a long, long time ago. I still remember how to milk a cow, gather eggs and plant for the harvest." He sighed as though he missed living on the farm.

"Come with me, Poor Boy, I'll show you where the tub is,

and get you a set of clean clothes. Mind, Shane's things may be a bit big on you but I think they'll do for now. If that's fine with you, Shane?" She waited for him to nod. "First, we need to get the water heated and then I'll stay with Shane while you take a bath." She frowned at the scowl on Poor Boy face, and when she glanced at Shane his lips were twitching as though he was trying to suppress a laugh. Her face heated as Shane winked at her. She turned on her heel and headed out the door with Poor Boy right behind her.

———

SHANE COULDN'T CONTAIN his laughter a minute more. If he was a betting man, he'd say that Poor Boy hadn't had a bath in at least a year. Perhaps under all that dirt he would finally be able to see just how old the boy was. Eats was probably having fits about now. The important thing was no one got hurt, of course. But how had the fire started? Once he was out of bed he'd have to find out if the town had a plan for fires.

He smiled as he listened to Cecily giving Poor Boy directions on how to take a bath. She was a kind and generous woman. They sure made a motley crew he, Cecily, and Poor Boy. He'd have Poor Boy take care of Jester as soon as he finished bathing.

When he heard Cecily's footsteps, he began to push himself up into a sitting position but damned himself from hell and back for being too damn weak. Laying his head back on the pillow, he waited for help. She set the coffee on the small table next to his bed.

"I know you're impatient and you're not the type to lay about, but stop trying to sit up by yourself." She leaned down and wrapped her arms around his chest and gently pulled him up until he was sitting. She smelled of vanilla and cinnamon, and her arms around him gave him a jolt he'd never felt before. If he wasn't so weak he'd have settled her into his arms and kissed her silly.

"Thank you, I appreciate all your help." He waited while Cecily fussed with his pillows and then leaned back against them. She handed him his cup of coffee, and he nodded his thanks. "I think this is the first bath Poor Boy's had in a year." He loved the way her lips curved into a smile.

"Shh, keep your voice down. We don't want to embarrass him. But I do think you're right. I bet he's very handsome under all that dirt." She took a sip of coffee. "It's very generous of you to allow him to stay."

Shane shrugged his shoulders. "It was all you're doing." He was surprised at the flash of panic on her face.

"If I overstepped, I'm sorry. I just couldn't say no."

"Cecily, have a seat and relax. You did nothing wrong. I would've done the same thing if I had answered the door. It's funny…a few days ago this house was empty, and now it's full. I like it full better. I was thinking he could take charge of Jester while I'm laid up."

Cecily sat in the chair next to the bed and nodded. "I wonder how long he's been with Eats?"

"Hard to say. The first time I saw him I thought Eats must be starving him to death but that wasn't the case at all. Eats gave him food and shelter and a job." He grinned. "Maybe you should go out there and make sure he's cleaning behind his ears." He laughed as quietly as he could as her eyes grew wide.

"Not until I know how old he is. I'd hate to think what Edith would say."

He reached out, took her hand and squeezed it, then loosened his grip but didn't let go. "Cecily… Don't base anything you do on what Edith would think. Don't allow that woman to poison your mind. I like you just the way you are. Did you know you look awfully pretty when you blush?" He rubbed his thumb over the back of her hand before he let it go.

"You shouldn't say things like that." She covered her reddened cheeks with her hands and turned from him. She was silent for a moment and then dropped her hands to her sides and faced him. "I work for you and that's all. I don't need compliments. I know what I am and how I must look to everyone. Somehow when people look at me they see a big stain on me. It's a stain that can't be removed. I don't see it when I look in the mirror. To me there is no stain, but there is a sad woman who looks back at me."

His heart ached at her words, and the wounded expression on her face made him promise to himself that he would always protect her. "I don't know what other people see when they look at you, but I see a capable, pretty, young woman. I've said this before and I'll say it again. You've got a lot of gumption. Most women would have just laid down and died, and for what? Just because of what other women would think? Tell you what, let's forget what other people think for a while."

She bit her lip and nodded her head but he wasn't convinced. She looked so unsure of herself, and it wasn't fair.

———

The next day Poor Boy came running into the house and into the bedroom practically out of breath. He looked like a different person with his shiny clean face and hair. Shane's clothes were much too big on the small body, but at least they were clean. She'd been right, he was younger than she had originally thought. She judged him to be about twelve years old, but when asked he refused to answer.

"There's some new lady that's come to see you, Sheriff. I

ain't never seen her before. Do you want me to run her off or what?"

Shane's brow furrowed as he glanced from Poor Boy to Cecily.

"I'll go see who it is." Cecily stood. "Don't you dare try to get out of bed." She gathered her wits about her and rushed to the front door feeling anxious. There stood a stunning woman dressed in the highest of fashion in her dark green traveling outfit with a matching hat all trimmed in the finest lace and ribbon. Her hair was dark almost black and her eyes were a lovely shade of brown.

"How do you do? My name is Lucy O'Connor and you are?" Lucy asked as she arched one eyebrow.

Cecily's heart sank. This must be Shane's wife. Why on earth hadn't he told anyone he was married? Disappointment floated through her as she realized she'd probably be sent packing soon. "I'm Cecily McGuinness I keep house for Sheriff O'Connor." She stepped back from the doorway. "Please come in. I'm sure you're worried about him, but he's doing just fine." Cecily led Lucy down the hall and motioned for her to go into the bedroom first.

Shane squinted then opened his eyes wide and smiled. "Is that really you, Lucy? How the heck did you end up in Asherville? I'd wondered how you fared and now you're here. My father?"

Lucy took off her hat, handed it to Cecily and then she sat on the wooden chair next to the bed fussing at the skirt of her dress. "Shane, I'm afraid I have bad news. Your father died about a year ago. I thought for sure you'd have been notified."

Shane heaved a sigh. "I had a feeling he was dead, but I didn't think trying to contact him would be good for either of us. When he told me to leave and never come back he meant it. I can still hear him saying it." Shane shook his head, his face looking drawn.

Cecily quickly glanced away from both of them, feeling like an intruder. She motioned to Poor Boy to come with her. She wondered if either she or Poor Boy would have a place to live since Mrs. O'Connor was now home where she belonged. She supposed she could take the boy and go back to Shannon's house, but Shannon was so close to her time, Cecily didn't want to cause any undue stress. Both Shannon and Addy were excellent examples of Pioneer women. They both worked with their husbands to build their ranches despite being in the family way.

"Why do you suppose she's here?" Poor Boy asked. "I guess I should look for another place to stay." His shoulders sagged as he sat at the kitchen table.

Cecily placed her hand on his shoulder and gave it a gentle squeeze. "I'm hoping it won't come to that."

"Come to what?" Lucy asked as she joined them in the kitchen.

"Poor Boy and I were wondering now that you're here to take care of Shane if we would have to leave. I'm sure you want to be alone with your husband."

"My dear, the house is a bit small, but I'm assuming you both work for the sheriff. As long as you do your work to my specifications, you have a place to stay. I would like some coffee now. You, boy, go get my bags and put them into Shane's room." Poor Boy quickly got to his feet and practically tripped as he raced out the front door.

Cecily poured coffee into a mug and handed it to Lucy, who sat at the table staring at the liquid. "You don't have many social graces do you? Don't you know enough to offer your guests cream and sugar with their coffee?"

Cecily's face heated and she bet it was bright red. "I do

have a bit of sugar but there's no cream. Would you like me to get you the sugar?"

"I wouldn't have asked if I didn't want it, and what do you mean there's no cream? Aren't you responsible for keeping up the kitchen as well as the rest of the house?"

Cecily put her right hand over her pounding heart. "Shane, did the shopping, and I guess he didn't think we needed cream."

Lucy's eyes narrowed. "To you, his name is either Mr. O'Connor or Sheriff O'Connor. You need to learn to show your employers more respect. Where exactly have you been sleeping?"

"Excuse me?"

"You heard me, and I'm waiting on your answer. In fact, I'm still waiting on the sugar."

Cecily felt as though she could hardly breathe-as if though the woman in the chair had taken all the oxygen out of the room. She found the sugar bowl and set it in front of Lucy along with a spoon. She stiffened as Lucy put four spoonful's of sugar into her coffee took a sip and pushed it away. Didn't she know how much sugar cost? "As for your answer as to where I sleep, I sleep in my own room."

Lucy stood and put her hands on her hip. "Show me."

Had Lucy been anyone else but Shane's wife Cecily would've told her to get out. She walked over to her room and opened the door. "This is my room."

Lucy shook her head. "Nothing in this house belongs to you. This is not your room it's just the room you've been sleeping in."

Upon hearing thuds and thumps coming from the front of the house, Cecily quickly turned away from Lucy and rushed to help Poor Boy with the luggage. It took both of them to carry the trunk into Shane's room. They set it down against the wall where Shane would not trip on it.

"What's that doing in here?" Shane's frown was as big as Texas.

"Mr. O'Connor, your wife instructed us to bring her belongings to your room. She does have a lot of luggage with her, and I hope it will all fit in here." Cecily didn't wait for a reply she was still hurt because Shane had never mentioned his wife. She grabbed another bag, brought it into the room and put it on top of the trunk.

"Cecily, I don't want her bags in here. And for the record, she's not my wife."

"Fine." She grabbed the bag and hauled it back out into the kitchen. Her mind was whirling. What did he mean Lucy wasn't his wife? What in the world was going on? "Poor Boy, let's go grab the trunk. Shane doesn't want it in his room." Poor Boy looked tired and annoyed, but he followed her.

"She ain't your wife?" he asked, scratching his jaw. "Are you sure cause she says she is. Did you get married and forget? Think hard, try to remember your wife. At least it don't look like you forgot any kids. Maybe you hit your head." Poor Boy looked so serious as he tried to be helpful, but by the thunderous look on Shane's face he wasn't helping at all.

"Poor Boy, do you think you could give Shane and me a moment alone? Leave the door open. I just have a few questions for him."

Poor Boy nodded and left.

"If you ask me I think it's Poor Boy who's been hit in the head one time too many," Shane said as he struggled to sit up.

"Oh no you don't." Cecily marched over and put her hands on his bare shoulders pushing him back onto the pillow. "You are to stay in bed. Would you like me to get you some of that laudanum? I heard it's good for calming nerves."

Shane stared at her his brow wrinkling. "Are you saying I'm not calm? I'll have you know I'm very calm, and no I don't want any of that laudanum. I need to keep my wits about me. Now what's this nonsense about Lucy being my wife?"

"That's what she said, and I'm to call you Mr. O'Connor or Sheriff O'Connor. She also suggested that if we didn't do our jobs we wouldn't be welcome to stay. Oh, and she likes cream with her coffee and lots and lots of sugar." Cecily paused and swallowed hard. "She wanted to see where I sleep so I happened to say my room and I was informed that it wasn't my room it was just the room I stay in. Is her last name even O'Connor" Cecily sat down in the chair and crossed her arms across her chest.

"Hell if I know. She's someone I grew up with. I want both you and Poor Boy to stay. Don't get it in your mind to run off. I'll have a talk with her and see what's going on. Have you got any food? I'm starved." He gave her a smile of reassurance.

She couldn't help but return his smile.

IF THE SITUATION hadn't been so serious Shane would've laughed long and hard. Imagine Poor Boy thought he'd forgotten he had a wife. Such was the stuff that good yarns were made of. He shook his head and wondered at Lucy's audacity. She probably took O'Connor as her last name when she was freed. It was his understanding that many of the slaves had taken the last name of the people that owned them.

As though he conjured her up, Lucy came into the bedroom and stood next to his bed. She tilted her head and sniffed as though she was upset.

Shane got straight to the point. "What's all this malarkey about you being my wife?"

"It was the safest way to travel, as your wife. No one wanted to mess with the wife of a sheriff. Besides, I didn't think you'd mind. You did tell me one time you wished you could marry me." She gave him what he hated most, a fake smile.

"Are you out of your mind? I liked you sure, but I never said I wanted to marry you. Why didn't you stop the ruse when you got to town? Why did you take it upon yourself to order Cecily and Poor Boy around? And why in God's name did you think you were going to share my room?"

"Well, I never." She grabbed a handkerchief from her sleeve and dabbed her eyes with it. "And all this time I thought you were pining away for me. That is why you left, isn't it? Your daddy wouldn't let you have me."

What could he say to that? She had been at the heart of his fight with his father, though not for the reasons she was hinting at.

"So you're passing." He shrugged his uninjured shoulder. "You do look lovely and very white. I suppose that made it easier for you to travel too."

She stiffened and her eyes flashed with anger. "You're not planning on telling anyone are you?"

He could tell she was holding her breath waiting for his answer. "I wouldn't do that to you. We'll just say we are distant cousins and childhood friends."

"Or you could just say I'm your wife. No one would question the wife of the sheriff." She gripped his shoulders to help him sit up.

Shane had a hard time catching his breath. "What are you doing? I've been shot in the shoulder."

Lucy shrugged and batted her eyelashes. "I was just trying to help you. I figured you'd want to be sitting up while we have our conversation. I'm sorry if I hurt you." She walked to the other side of the bed and sat in the wooden chair. "Really,

Shane, you must do something about the furniture you have in your house. It looks like a collection of pieces that someone was throwing away."

"The chair you're sitting in was made by my friend Keegan. He's good at what he does. Things are different out here. This isn't the South where everything was opulent. Here we all have to carry our weight or we don't eat. It's a different way of life, but I'm sure you'll get used to it. We'll have a cow, some chickens, and a few pigs pretty soon. We're also going to put in a garden and grow our own food. I know I can count on you to help." He breathed in deeply trying not to laugh at the shock and annoyance on her face. Did she think that white people didn't work? If so she was in for a rude awakening. He wasn't sure he liked the idea of her passing for white. People were bound to kill her if they found out.

She pasted another fake smile on her face and nodded. "Why a little farm sounds like fun," she said in a syrupy voice. "You do know that I always worked in the house, and I have no knowledge of critters or gardening."

Grinning widely Shane stared at her. "Well it's about time you learned. How's your cooking?"

Lucy sputtered and shook her head. "You have servants for that."

"They are not servants. They're friends who have hit a bump in the road. We plan to work together to get the farm started. I'm sure you can take turns cooking the meals, doing the laundry and anything else that needs doing." Lucy narrowed her eyes and gave him a mulish look. He could tell she was going to be nothing but trouble. Lots and lots of trouble.

Cecily poked her head in and caught Shane's gaze. "Are you hungry? We really should try to get some food in you.

And I also need to sponge you down, you still have a fever." Lucy gasped and put her right hand over her heart.

"I'd appreciate it, Cecily," Shane said.

Cecily nodded. "I'll be right back." She gave him a sweet smile, and he couldn't help but compare her genuine caring to Lucy's selfishness.

"You allow her to bathe you? Why that little hussy. Just how long has she been working for you? It can't be good for your reputation to have such a woman around."

A gasp came from the doorway. Cecily stood there, looking wan. Damn she'd heard Lucy's words.

He smiled at her. "Something smells good."

"Why, it's my new perfume," Lucy said.

Shane shook his head. "I meant the food." He watched as Cecily entered the room carrying a wooden tray laden with a light meal. No matter what, Cecily brightened every room she entered and he admired her.

"Lucy, would you mind moving so I can set the tray on the table?"

Lucy hesitated so long Shane thought she would refuse.

At last, she stood with her nose practically in the air. "I wouldn't want to get in the way of your duties."

Cecily's expression was cold as she put the food on the table. She turned, ready to sit down and help Shane, but Lucy grabbed the chair, pulled it to the other side of the bed and sat.

"I think I can take it from here. I'd advise you to knock before you enter again."

It hurt that Cecily didn't even glance at him for confirmation of Lucy's words before she left the room. Surely she must know Lucy's words meant nothing. He sighed of course she didn't know and it was his fault for not setting things straight.

"Lucy you can't take it upon yourself to give direction to

anyone in this house." Her eyes narrowed as she nodded. "I mean it."

"Yes, I'm sure you do."

———

HUMILIATION SWEPT THROUGH CECILY, heating her face. She sat down at the kitchen table and covered her cheeks with her hands hoping to cool them. She had felt assured by Shane's earlier words, but his actions told a different story. He could have intervened with Lucy, but he hadn't. In fact, he hadn't seemed surprised by her at all. The last few days had been lovely, but now it was back to reality.

She sighed and dropped her hands. At least she wasn't making money flat on her back. She and Poor Boy had a place to live and food to fill their bellies. Lord knew they'd both been through worse.

Poor Boy entered the house, dragging his feet. "Jester is all set. There's no swelling in his foot, and he seems to be standing right. He's really a great horse. It's been a long time since I've been around horses but I love them. I know they don't talk but you can tell by the way they look at you and by their ears what they are saying."

"Their ears?"

Poor Boy gave her a shy grin and nodded. "If they pin their ears back they're not happy, and you need to be on your toes. If they are listening, you can tell by the way their ears turn a bit in your direction."

"Poor Boy, where did you learn so much about horses?"

The boy turned red and pretended to examine the wooden floor. "My pa he taught me before he died. Then my ma got remarried. Her husband was big and mean with powerful fists. He used those fists on my mom on me and on the horses. I had a horse of my own named Horizon. He was the best horse ever, and that awful man shot him in the head for no reason. I begged my mom to leave, but she refused, so I took off before he could shoot me in the head too." Poor Boy sat down at the table and folded his arms on it before laying his head down.

Cecily's heart broke for him. No wonder he had nightmares. She wanted to ask him how old he really was but decided not to pry. She had a feeling he'd confide in her again. "I'm so sorry, Poor Boy. Life isn't fair and bad things happen to good people like you and me. I don't have any answers as to why. I've asked God over and over again, why me. I never seem to get an answer or maybe I don't recognize the answer. They say God works in mysterious ways such as giving us a place here with Shane."

"I ain't talked to God in a very long time. Do you think he's forgotten about me?"

"I'm no expert but I don't think he forgets about anyone. Are you hungry?" She laughed. "Of course you are. I don't even know why I asked."

He lifted his head his eyes shining and the corners of his mouth were turned up. "You're right I'm starving."

THE DAY WAS TURNING out to be a very trying. Cecily's hand twitched to slap the smug look off Lucy's face. Lucy only came out of Shane's room by necessity otherwise she planted herself on the chair next to Shane's bed not offering to help. Asking her constantly to move out of the way grew tiresome. It also irked Cecily to no end the way Lucy stared at her while she wiped down Shane with cool water. If Lucy was such a good friend of Shane's, perhaps she could wash him down.

Shaking her head, Cecily sighed and sat down at the

kitchen table. Poor Boy seemed to be at loose ends and was trying anything to stay out of Lucy's way. The doctor would be there soon, and she wondered how Lucy would act in front of him. Then there would be the problem of who slept where. She supposed she'd have to give up her bedroom, so Lucy would have a nice place to sleep. She wouldn't have minded one bit giving up her room; it was the fact that Lucy would be sleeping there that made her mad.

Cecily smiled, she'd spent so much time being angry with Lucy, she'd forgotten how frightened she usually was. Perhaps there was hope for her after all. A knock at the door startled her, and she thought herself hopeless once again as she quickly went to see who it was. Opening the door, she smiled at the doctor and Edith.

"Welcome, I'm so glad to see you both." She stepped aside to allow the newcomers to enter.

"How's the patient?" the doctor asked.

"He still has a fever, but I was able to get him to eat."

"So you fed him? I had visions of him starving." Edith frowned as she put a big basket on the kitchen table. "I brought him something edible."

Cecily didn't acknowledge the barb.

The doctor cleared his throat. "Well I'll just go on in to see the patient." Cecily nodded, wondering what type of reception he'd get from Lucy.

She watched as he walked to the threshold, peered in, and frowned.

The doctor stepped into the room. "I didn't know you had company."

Edith's eyes widened as she hurried to Shane's room. Cecily couldn't help but grin as she followed. She caught the tail end of Shane's introduction and watched while the doctor gave Lucy a stoic nod.

Edith's mouth dropped open as her eyes narrowed. "How do you two know each other?"

Lucy turned and stared at Edith giving her a haughty look. "Why we've been friends since we were children. We practically grew up together. I'm sure you've heard how bad things are in the South. So here I am visiting with my oldest friend."

Cecily tried not to smile. Just maybe Edith had met her match. She did notice however, that Lucy did not stand to greet either the doctor or Edith.

"Well, I'll examine the patient if that is alright with you, Shane?"

Shane nodded.

Edith turned to leave but when she noticed that Lucy intended to stay she shook her head. "Come on, Lucy, dear I'm sure they want their privacy." Edith crossed her arms in front of her and tapped her foot.

Lucy scowled as she stood. She took a moment to pat her hair in place and to smooth out her skirt. "I'll be right outside my dear, Shane, if you need me." She practically waltzed out of the room.

Edith stared at Cecily with wide eyes but Cecily merely shrugged her shoulders.

Spotting Poor Boy, Edith smiled. "I'm glad you found somewhere to stay, I was worried about you."

Poor Boy gave Edith a slight nod and ducked his head. "I get to stay as long as I like."

"Shane is a good person," Edith said. "There's fried chicken in that basket if you'd like. Help yourself." Edith smiled as Poor Boy reached in and took a leg.

"I'd offer tea in the parlor but as you can see the house is barely furnished and there doesn't seem to be any tea," Lucy explained to Edith.

"I suppose Shane could use a few more pieces of furniture, but he's not here much. Why, I doubt he sees any need since he doesn't use the front two rooms." Edith turned her back on Lucy. "Cecily, how has he been? Has his fever gotten worse?"

Lucy walked until she was in Edith's line of sight. "I don't know why you're asking her. I've been taking care of Shane. I think he still has a slight fever, but it's hard to tell with someone constantly interrupting us to wash him down with cold water. It's highly improper."

Cecily didn't get a chance to open her mouth.

"Well if you're by his side, why is it considered improper? She's just bathing his face, arms and chest. Is there something else going on I need to know about?" Edith stared at Lucy and then at Cecily.

Cecily decided not to say a word and to let Lucy handle it.

"It's hardly seemly," Lucy said. "She hasn't known Shane for very long."

Edith gave Lucy a pointed stare. "Would you rather Shane die? If you thought it so improper why weren't you cooling his fever?"

Lucy blinked a few times and shook her head. "I'm not the hired help." She turned and walked back to the table and sat down. "I would like a cup coffee, and don't skimp on the sugar this time."

"Edith, would you like a cup of coffee too?" Cecily offered.

"Thank you, Cecily, I would love a cup of coffee." Edith walked over to the table and Poor Boy pulled out her chair for her. Cecily saw the glare Lucy gave Poor Boy. There would be no peace in the house tonight.

Cecily got the coffee ready making sure she set out the sugar bowl for Lucy. She placed Edith's coffee on the table first and then placed Lucy's in front of her. She poured another cup and handed it to Poor Boy who backed himself into one corner of the room. Finally, she got a cup of coffee for herself and placed it on the table. She started to pull out the chair.

Lucy made a huffing noise. "You don't expect to sit with us do you? Hired help never sits with their betters."

Edith drew in a deep breath as her hand went over her chest. "Cecily, sit down." She turned and gazed at Lucy. "We don't do things out here the same way you did in the South. We don't believe in slaves or indentured servants. It's not practical to have Cecily eat or sit at a different table. Most of us are not blessed with extra help. Texas isn't a place for genteel women. In order to survive out west everyone, and I mean everyone, needs to pull their own weight. Oh sure, there's the ones with money and the ones without, but at the end of the day if there's a problem we pull together. Cecily comes from a good home and upbringing. She grew up on a farm in Pennsylvania, and her knowledge of farming is an asset to our community. She's definitely an asset to Shane, who plans on building a small farm. Now, Poor Boy has been in town for many years." She bestowed a glance on Cecily. "By the way, you've done a good job cleaning him up." Then Edith turned toward Poor Boy. "You look real nice."

His face bloomed crimson and he nodded then cast his eyes to the floor.

"Now where was I? Oh yes, Poor Boy. There has not been a day when Poor Boy hasn't worked for a place to stay and food to eat. He never causes any trouble, and I'm glad Shane took him in. It'll take a bit of time for you, Lucy, to get acquainted with our way of life. It's best to keep your haughty manner to yourself."

Cecily had to keep her jaw from dropping. Did Edith just defend her and Poor Boy? Things certainly weren't boring in Asherville. Cecily nodded her thanks to Edith and winked at Poor Boy.

Lucy sat in the chair straight and tall with a slight lift to her chin. She added four teaspoons of sugar into her coffee, picked up the spoon and stirred it, acting as though she hadn't heard anything Edith had to say. Secretly, Cecily was delighted to have the bull's-eye taken off her back and placed on Lucy's.

"So, what is it you do in town, Edith? I'm assuming you have a job."

"Why, I own the mercantile," Edith said with pride.

Lucy waved her hand as though shooing away a fly. "So you're in trade. How nice for you. You probably know everything that goes on in town. Are there committees or groups of women who do not have to work for a living?"

Edith shook her head and arched her eyebrow. "I'm sure you can make all the committees and groups you like, but I think you'll find the membership of each will be one. The only woman of substance in our town is Addy Quinn She comes from a rich family in Boston but you would never know. She treats everyone as an equal and hasn't used her immense inheritance on fancy clothes and other fripperies. She's put a fair amount into the ranch she and her husband own. They don't make them nicer than Addy."

Cecily got up and grabbed the coffee pot refilling everyone's cup before she sat down. "How are Addy and Shannon?"

Edith smiled. "Both have been declared under house arrest by their husbands. Those two scamps wanted to come and help you with Shane. They will both feel better knowing that you have Poor Boy to help you."

Cecily nodded and smiled.

"Well, I'm here now," Lucy declared. "I don't see the need for us all to be here. Cecily, perhaps could go and work for this Addy or that Shannon. I'm sure you could take Poor Boy along. I'll take care of Shane."

Cecily laughed and shook her head. She couldn't help her laughter and had to cover her mouth with her hand. Finally, she managed to get control of herself and stopped. "I saw your way of taking care of Shane. Staring at him impatiently and then talking him to death when he's awake is not how you nurse a person. I never once saw you get him a glass of water or wipe his brow. And as far as talking nonstop, all you do is tire him out."

Lucy scowled and narrowed her eyes as she stared at Cecily. "I don't take kindly to servants talking to me in such a tone. A good whipping would teach you your place. And, Edith, thank you for your unsolicited advice. I'm staying, and I'm running the house the way I want. Now, Cecily, remove yourself from the table."

Cecily was torn. She didn't know what to do. If she showed weakness now, she'd never gain the upper hand, yet would Lucy really have her whipped.? How Shane could have a friend such as Lucy she'd never know.

The doctor walked into the kitchen, smiling. "I do believe he's going to be just fine. Cecily keep doing what you been doing. It's working. He does seem a bit tuckered out. It's not unusual for person who's gunshot to take several naps during the day. Raised voices, fighting and overall tension are not good for him. I'll be back tomorrow. Miss Edith, may I walk you home?"

"Thanks, Doc, I'll take you up on your offer. I'll be back tomorrow." Edith gave Lucy a malicious smile.

Cecily walked ahead of the couple and opened the door for them.

"You stay clear of that viper. I've dealt with women like her before. Don't you worry. Like I said I'll be here tomorrow," Edith said with a stiff nod as she took the doc's arm and went down the stairs.

For a moment, Cecily wished she could leave. All she

wanted in life was peace, and she'd had it, but for such a brief time she wanted more. Lucy was going to find out the hard way that she took all threats seriously and she wasn't afraid to fight back. She'd probably have to defend Poor Boy too, but she'd learned a lot being Long Nose's wife. Fighting to inflict pain was the only way to fight and she was up for it. She just hoped it wouldn't come to that.

SHANE DREAMED he was swimming in a secluded pond filled with cool water. It felt so good to dive in and just swim. The only thing that could've made it better was if he wasn't alone. His eyes blinked as he awakened. He sighed, wishing he could go back into his dream until he turned his head and glimpsed Cecily by his side sitting in the ladder back chair, sound asleep. She really was lovely with her thick shiny sable hair flowing around her shoulders. She had on the yellow dress he'd bought for her, and the color looked very good on her. She brightened the room with her presence. Every once in awhile she would snore, and he wanted to laugh out loud. He'd bet the farm she didn't know.

He sighed as he gazed at her lovely complexion with her skin so fair and so soft. Her high cheekbones were rosy, and her lips looked like luscious bows or perhaps cherries was a better description. He liked seeing her at peace. There were many times he saw a flicker of pain cross her face and wondered what she was thinking or remembering. She'd been through an ordeal many didn't survive, and it made him mad that people looked down on her now. They should be congratulating her on her bravery but instead they wanted to know why she didn't kill herself. He shook his head. He'd never understand people. He glanced around wondering what time it was. The bedroom door was open and he could see sunlight in the kitchen. A lot had happened in such a short time. Getting shot was unexpected and so was Lucy's arrival. He had been certain he'd never see her again, yet somehow she'd found him. She probably had all types of opportunities for marriage, yet here she was in Asherville.

He shook his head. She was right; they'd been the best of friends growing up, and Lucy was one of the reasons he'd left the South for good. It wasn't anything romantic, but he was afraid that in Lucy's mind it was. Shane never liked the notion of slavery, and he and his father often argued. But his father was right, he couldn't maintain his way of life without free labor. If that was the way it had to be, Shane wanted no part of it. Lucy had been looking at him with wide eyes and possibly big dreams, and Shane's father didn't like that. In fact, he had been making arrangements to sell Lucy, and ultimately that was the reason Shane left and headed west.

He really didn't have any plan in mind, didn't know where he was going or what he was going to do, but he had two good hands and a strong back, and that was all he needed. He was good with the gun, but he didn't want to be known for being a quick draw. That type of thing got men killed, and he expected to be around for a good while yet.

He tried to sit up and ended up groaning, waking Cecily from her slumber.

"Oh my, I'm supposed to be taking care of you and here I am sleeping on the job," she said with a trace of humor in her voice. Reaching over she placed her hand on his forehead and smiled. "Well, Sheriff O'Connor, I do believe you'll survive. Your fever is gone, and I'd say that's a good sign."

"It's all thanks to you and your wonderful care." He smiled as he gazed at her.

"Oh bother, you two can stop right there Shane," Lucky said as she barged into the room. "You fell asleep, so you have no idea that I was the one who took on the responsibility of your care. Are you hungry? I'm sure we can have Cecily whip up something for you."

Cecily's shoulders slumped, and any good cheer she'd had drained from her. He was pretty sure it had been Cecily, not Lucy, who had nursed him back to health.

"How long have I been out? Has it been a few days?"

"No, the doctor just left about three hours ago," Cecily told him as she gave Lucy a pointed stare.

"Then I'm confused. Lucy, when was it you nursed me back to health? Seems to me Cecily has done all the work."

Lucy dismissed him with a flick of her hand. "You were sleeping, so you don't know a thing. I'm glad I was here and that you're now well."

Cecily stood and walked toward the doorway. She stopped and looked back toward Shane. "You're not well. We've only climbed over the first hurdle, your fever. So you stay in bed." She quickly turned away and was out the door.

Shane smiled widely.

"What's that smile for? Don't tell me you've fallen for the help."

Shane stared at the ugly frown on Lucy's face. "I was just thinking that for such a tiny woman, she sure is bossy. She's fearless all right." He nodded and kept smiling until Lucy glared at him.

"Well as long as she realizes she's not in charge here, we should all get along just fine."

"Listen, Lucy, I don't want to fight with you, but I do remember not too long ago that *you* were the help. I'm sure you wished you'd been treated with kindness and respect. Cecily isn't any more of a servant here than you are. Texas is a place where you have to work to survive."

She jutted out her bottom lip as she crossed her arms in front of her. "So that's how it is. I should've known, but somehow I missed all the clues."

Puzzled, Shane tried to make sense of what she was saying. "What clues are you talking about?"

"I see the way you look at her and how you hang on her every word. But from what I've gathered she's not a fit wife... for you or any other man." She sat on the edge of the bed and touched his hand. "Don't you remember what we were to each other? How much we felt for each other? How we longed for each other? I know that's why you left."

Shane drew his hand from her grasp and groaned as he tried to move to the other side of the bed. "Lucy, we were childhood friends and that was it. There was no longing for each other, at least not on my part. I'm sorry if somehow I misled you."

"Misled me?" Lucy stood and paced at the end of the bed. "We were destined to be together everyone said so. I grew up knowing I was yours, and I couldn't wait for the day when we could be together. You seem to have forgotten how much you loved me."

"I don't know where you got the idea that we could ever be together. I left before the War Between the States, when you were still a slave. Just how did you think we were going to be together?"

She stopped her pacing and stiffened as she turned and stared at him with tears in her eyes. "I waited and waited for you to come to me, but you never did. I knew in my heart that someday you would take me to be your mistress. But now I'm free, and we could be married if you wanted to. There's no one here to say I'm not white. Shane, you need to look into your heart and remember how it was between us before you left. Do you remember when you taught me how to dance? Didn't it feel good to be in each other's arms? Why we spent so much time together I never imagined you leaving without me. You left me alone to the ridicule of all the slaves who said I was uppity and needed to be brought down a peg or two. I still worked in the house but every night I went back to my cabin and was alone." A tear trailed down her face.

"You know there's always been a division between the house slaves and the others. I don't think it was because I left. I think it was because you acted as though you were better than the others. It doesn't matter what your station in life is, you should always have compassion for others less fortunate than you. I know you had plenty of proposals but you turned them all down. My father saw the way you looked at me and planned to sell you. You would have been ripped away from your family."

Shane ran his fingers through his hair and shook his head. "We argued, and my father said if I didn't like the way he ran things I was welcome to leave. I packed that very night and left the next morning. I left before he had the chance to sell you. I didn't feel that way about you and I refused to be the reason you were sold. I don't believe in one person owning another, but I could've kept my beliefs to myself if it weren't for the cruelty of beatings and the selling of a slave's family members."

Her jaw dropped open, and she gazed at him as though he was someone she didn't know. "I saw the lust in your eyes every time you looked at me. It thrilled me to no end, and I was dying of anticipation to be with you."

"I never meant to hurt you, but what you're saying simply isn't true. I also don't believe in masters bedding their slaves."

Her eyes narrowed. "You could've bought me. I'm sure your daddy would've given you a good price. That's what I could not understand all these years is why you left me. I tried every which way for us to be friends."

"And you succeeded. We were the best of friends when we were children, but you must have known that our lives were going down different paths. I might have left suddenly, but I would have left eventually. It wasn't my dream to be a plantation owner, and my father knew it. He told me more than once how disappointed he was in me. So I'm glad I left, and I'm glad I found this little town where people are valued based on their work ethic and not for how much money they have in the bank."

Lucy shook her head. "How can you say that? You have one of the nicest houses in the whole damn town. Wasn't there a lesser house you could have purchased?"

"Not that it's any of your business but this was one of the few houses available. The life of the sheriff can be short or long. You just never know. I just wanted someplace of my own to hang my hat."

Lucy glanced at the door before she glanced back at him giving him a smile. "I love you, Shane O'Connor, and I know deep down you love me and always have." She walked toward the door and stopped. "Cecily, I didn't see you there. You really shouldn't eavesdrop on conversations. It's impolite."

CECILY DIDN'T KNOW what to think but it pained her heart to hear Lucy's words of their love. It really wasn't any of her business; she just worked for Shane. Lucy was a very attractive woman and she couldn't blame Shane for loving her. Disappointment floated through her. She couldn't help her feelings even if she had no right to them. She stepped back out of Lucy's way and watched her walk out the front door. Taking a deep breath she walked into Shane's room trying to keep a smile on her face. "Is there anything you need?"

His eyes gentled as he gazed at her and after a fashion, the ends of his mouth turned up. "How's Poor Boy getting along? I want him to feel at home here. But I have an inkling you've done that."

Her face heated at his praise and she smiled back. "He's a good kid, smart too. Do you think it would be okay if I tried teaching him to read? I don't want to overstep my bounds here. The whole situation is new for all of us and I suppose we'll each have to find our way. Right now, I'm just hoping we can all get along."

Shane's smile grew deeper until his dimples showed. "That's what I like about you. You're always thinking of others first. I've traveled the country, and I have to tell you it's a rare quality. I'm not sure what we're going to do about the sleeping arrangements. I'll give up my room so Lucy doesn't pitch a fit if she doesn't have her own bedroom. I was thinking we could turn the two front rooms into bedrooms. I see no other use for them anyway. But for now I can make a pallet in front of the stove."

She put her hands on her hips "You're right no one wants to see her pitch a fit. Poor Boy and I are grateful to have a roof over our heads and food to fill our stomachs. It doesn't much matter where we sleep. We'd be happy to sleep out here. You are not well enough to give up your room. Don't worry about Lucy, I've already begun to ignore her less than pleasant statements. She's very beautiful, and from what I understand you were childhood sweethearts. Starting tomorrow, I'll look around for another place to stay. I don't want you getting upset. It's the right thing to do."

Shane patted the side of his bed, offering her a place to sit. Cecily hesitated then sat next to him. She arched her eyebrow in surprise as he took her hand in his. "You're not leaving and neither is Poor Boy. We're going to have that farm we've been talking about. It's getting late, but in the morning have Poor Boy come in and talk to me. I want to know what skills he might possess. Who knows? He might be able to make a chicken coop, but we'll see. If not, then we can hire someone. Are you sure you want to be tied down to a farm? There are no days off. The animals have to be fed and cared for."

A wave of anticipation washed over her. Having animals and planting a garden would make her feel more grounded, as though she belonged. But she'd have to keep herself from getting too attached. Whether he knew it or not, Lucy had big plans for him.

"I'm sure, and I'll stay as long as you'll have me. I can't promise Poor Boy will stay, though. I have a feeling if Eats opens up another restaurant, Poor Boy will want to be by his side."

"Understandable. It seems as though Poor Boy views Eats as a father figure. And you're not bound to the property either. I'm sure some man will come to sweep you off your feet and steal you from me."

She ducked her head and gently withdrew her hand from his, not knowing what to say or do. There'd be no man ever. The silence became awkward, and she put on her best false smile and stood. "I'll get the sleeping arrangements all set. I'll be back to check on you as soon as I'm done. I'm sorry you're stuck in bed. I can tell you're not the type who likes to stay still for very long. I'm sure after we all get to know each other better everything will run smoothly."

Shane laughed. "In this case, I think you're being overly optimistic, but if we all try, it might be bearable."

"I'll see you in a little bit. Try to get some rest." She went out the door and quietly closed it behind her. He was probably right about her being optimistic, but she had to try for all their sakes. She had a feeling that being on the wrong side of Lucy would be a living hell.

CHAPTER FOUR

*T*he next day didn't start cheerfully at all. Cecily had an ache in her neck from sleeping in the chair in Shane's room. Despite the pain and Lucy's glare she made them all breakfast and decided a simple fare of beef broth would be perfect for the evening meal. Shane hadn't eaten much breakfast and she wanted something that would be easy on his stomach.

Before he was even done chewing his food, Poor Boy was out the door. Cecily longed to go with him. Lucy didn't say much but it was her manner that had Cecily on edge. Lucy stared at her and shook her head most of the morning until Cecily's nerves were frayed. Of course as soon as the dishes needed to be washed, Lucy had grabbed her shawl and left.

Cecily cleaned the kitchen and checked on Shane who had fallen back to sleep. She needed a breath of fresh air and decided to join Poor Boy out at the barn.

It was windy, very windy, and she had a hard time trying to keep her dress in place. It was a good thing she wasn't going anywhere important. Her hair flew all around her head. The barn look sturdy enough, not as new as the house, but much better than some she'd seen. She smiled. They'd be able to have a good farm here. She stopped just before the barn door and glanced over the parcel of land that Shane owned. In her mind's eye she could picture chickens, pigs, a dog or two, a big garden, and a crop to bring in some money. She'd have to find out what type of crops grew best out here. Things were bound to be very different from Pennsylvania.

She threw open the barn door and stepped inside. It took a moment for her eyes to adjust to the darkness. Jester was in the first stall and he neighed at her in greeting. She crossed over to Jester and patted his fine face. "How you doing, Boy? You're looking good. Poor Boy seems to be doing a fine job of taking care of you." She glanced inside the stall and saw that the horse had plenty of hay and clean water.

She looked into the empty stall next to Jester and was surprised to see Poor Boy sleeping on a mound of hay with an old worn wool blanket full of holes over him. He was such a good kid and she certainly didn't begrudge the nap he was taking. Keeping silent, she left the barn, eased the door closed against the wind, and started back toward the house. Glancing left, she caught sight of a figure at the entrance of the hidden trail in the canyon. Fear held her in place for the barest minute before she ran back into the barn.

"Poor Boy, come quick I think trouble is headed our way. Let's make our way inside as quickly as we can."

He woke and was on his feet instantly. He scrambled out of the stall and followed her to the door. He watched while Cecily peeked out and then he ran with her across the yard and into the house.

"Poor Boy, I need you to keep watch out the front window." She led him to one of the front windows and pointed out the man in the canyon. "Keep an eye on him while I go fetch the guns. I don't know most people who live around here and it's better safe than sorry. If you recognize him holler to me."

Cecily ran from window to window quickly closing the shutters. She grabbed the rifle which was placed on the mantle over the fireplace. She didn't know where the shells were. Rushing into Shane's room she was practically out of breath when she asked him where the ammunition was.

"Whoa, darlin', what's got you so upset?"

"There's a man coming from the secret trail. I know how to shoot. I need ammunition for the rifle and I need your gun."

Shane groaned as he tried to sit up. "Here help me up and grab a shirt for me. Don't argue with me I can sit in the chair by the front window with my gun."

Cecily nodded and quickly helped him to sit up while she hurriedly helped him into his shirt. She grabbed his arm and placed it over her shoulders and led him out to the front room. She left him leaning against the wall as she ran to grab a wooden chair for him.

Perspiration formed on Shane's brow. "The shotgun shells and bullets for my gun are under my bed. My gun belt is draped over my headboard. Run and get them for me, Poor Boy."

Poor Boy nodded and ran.

Cecily stood behind Shane and pointed out the man in the canyon. "Do you know him?"

Shane looked out the window for a bit before he shook his head.

"Can't rightly say I do. Lucy isn't back yet?"

"No, she hasn't been gone very long at all. She said she was going to the mercantile but who knows. Poor Boy, please hurry."

"I got them, I got all you asked for." Poor Boy skidded to a stop right next to Shane's chair. "I never seen that man before have you, Shane? I'll take the rifle if you want the gun."

Cecily widened her eyes in surprise. "I'm a pretty good shot myself you know," she said.

Poor Boy stared at Shane waiting for him to make a decision.

"Poor Boy, I'm gonna need you to reload. I know you're fast and I need someone fast. Same goes for Cecily she'll need someone fast to help her too. Now no shooting until we see what this varmint wants. But it wouldn't hurt to be ready. Cecily, do you have anyone coming after you? What about you, Poor Boy?"

Cecily felt all color drain from her face, and it took all she had not to sway.

"Oh damn," he said quickly. "I'm sorry, both of you. Of course you've had awful people in your life. It was just the sheriff in me asking those questions. I didn't mean to make you feel uncomfortable or to blame either of you."

Cecily nodded and grabbed the gun. She checked it and made sure it was fully loaded before she went to the other window. Looking out the shutter hole she kept an eye on the stranger. Breathing became labored as her fear grew. Didn't the man know that this was the Sheriff's house? Time dragged as they waited for the man to get closer. He didn't look dangerous in his nice clothes. He looked to be the same age as Shane, and he certainly seemed out of place.

"Well, I'll be damned." Shane shook his head. "We can put our guns down. Poor Boy why don't you open the door for me? Don't worry, we're safe. It's my old friend Elliott McManus from back home."

Poor Boy seemed stuck to the floor; he didn't move. Cecily set down the gun and opened the door, hoping—praying—Shane was right. The man smiled, and his eyes lit up as he tipped his hat at her. "Ma'am, it's mighty nice to see you. My name is Elliott, Elliott McManus, and I'm looking for a man named Shane O'Connor," he drawled with a deep southern accent.

Cecily stiffened as her eyes narrowed. "Now what would you be wanting with the sheriff?"

Elliott's green eyes filled with humor as he tipped back his head and laughed. "I do believe it's another Shane O'Connor I'm looking for. The man I'm searching for went out of his way to taunt the authorities when we were kids."

"Oh bother, just come in. Shane's been shot, and I have to get him back into bed. You look like you have a strong back and you'll be of some help."

Elliott was still laughing as he entered the house. His smile grew wider as he approached Shane and slapped him on the shoulder causing Shane to yelp in pain.

"Oh hell, oh excuse me, ma'am, I meant heck. Did I just hit you where you were shot? Figures. I've had a hell of a time finding you."

Shane shook his head and his eyes filled with humor. "Good to see you, Elliott. I've never thought I'd see you in Texas of all places. Here, give an old friend some help back into the bed. I'm just as glad I didn't have to shoot that rifle. It's got quite a kick to it."

Cecily and Poor Boy watched Elliott help Shane into the bedroom. There was lots of laughter with a groan and a moan mixed in. Poor Boy looked at her and shrugged his shoulders. "I guess we're safe, Cecily. Thank you for coming to get me."

She tilted her head and studied Poor Boy. It was as though no one ever gave him a second thought. "You don't have to thank me. We're practically family."

"Family...yep, you can be my family any time, Cecily." He made himself busy picking up the firearms and ammunition and then he headed into Shane's room.

Her heart still beat out of control, and there would be no calming it. Just when she thought she might be able to relax, Elliott McManus came as a reminder that she'd always have to watch her back. What was he doing coming through the canyon wall? Where was his horse? Shane would get answers.

She assembled the ingredients to make bread and commenced making the dough. The kitchen grew uncomfortably warm, and she pushed back a few strands of hair that had loosened, positive she'd had gotten flour in her hair. Not that it mattered, for there was no one to see her. After all, she was just the hired help.

Funny how, until Lucy showed up, being hired help had been a good thing, an honorable thing, and she had been grateful. Actually, she was happy to have a job and a roof over her head. Picking up a cloth, she wiped her hands and shook her head. Her happiness had been stripped from her one too many times, and there was no way she would allow Lucy to strip it away again. She had survived. After all, that was what she did best, survive. Looking into the small mirror, she dabbed the flour from her hair. She tried every waking moment to forget the atrocities she had suffered at the hands of Long Nose. She covered the loaves of bread with cloths so they would rise. If she kept herself busy doing chores, the probability of being around Lucy would be low.

She'd expected Poor Boy to hightail it out of Shane's bedroom. He was never comfortable around strangers. To her amazement Poor Boy remained in Shane's bedroom. She poured herself a glass of water and went out onto the porch for fresh air. The surroundings were so peaceful and serene, it was hard to believe that they had been scrambling for cover less than an hour ago. Texas certainly was unpredictable country and so very different from Pennsylvania.

She wondered how her mama and daddy were doing on

the farm. It was a meager existence, but they had refused to move, citing the generations of McGuinnesses who had worked the land before them. A wave of homesickness washed over her, and she wished she had stayed on the farm. It would have prevented a lot of pain and heartache, but there was no going back now. No matter how much Mama and Daddy loved her, they'd still see her as tainted.

In the distance she spotted Lucy walking at the edge of town. She had a strange way of walking; she kept her head up but it appeared as though she avoided all eye contact. Odd she had no problem eyeing Cecily with that pointed stare. Shrugging her shoulders, she turned and walked back into the house. Lucy was none of her business, and she planned to keep it that way.

SHANE COULDN'T REMEMBER SMILING SO MUCH. It was damn good to see his old friend. Though the news from home wasn't so good. The plantation had been overrun. Those good for nothing Yankees, winning wasn't enough for them they'd had to pillage and plunder the whole of the South. Unfortunately, that was the way of war.

"I'm sorry the news from home couldn't have been better. You were right to leave when you did. I just wish I'd done the same," Elliott said as he eyed Poor Boy who was sitting in the corner pretending not to listen to their conversation.

Shane nodded and gritted his teeth, wishing he had the words to make everything alright again. The life they'd known growing up was now gone, forever. For all of Elliott's bravado Shane saw a flicker of being lost in Elliott's eyes. "Now, we forge on and make new lives for ourselves. Being sheriff is something I fell into, but I like it. I like the town and its people. Some have become like family to me."

Elliott rubbed the back of his neck and gave Shane a feeble smile. "You're right our lives can be anything we make them. I haven't quite decided what I'm going to do. Truthfully, I followed you here to Asherville once I picked up your trail. I really don't have much of a plan." Elliott shrugged. "I don't suppose there's many positions for a plantation owner in these here parts. Hell, all I know is how to grow cotton. Though I have to say, I've heard about your Texas Longhorns, and I'd love to see one."

"It's hard work, but a rancher's life can be rewarding. I have two friends who are ranchers. Cinders and Keegan have both built nice lives for themselves and their wives. In fact, we've been waiting on news haven't we, Poor Boy?" Shane stared at Poor Boy until he finally looked up. Poor Boy gave him a quick nod. "Both their wives are expecting, and their time is near."

"I'll have to give it some thought and check out ranching and all. So tell me how you got so lucky as to have someone as fine as Cecily working for you?"

Poor Boy's eyes widened. "She don't like being talked about. But I tell you one thing, she's the nicest lady I know."

"That has to be the best compliment I have ever received. Thank you, Poor Boy," Cecily said as she smiled at Poor Boy. "I didn't mean to interrupt I just wanted to know if you needed anything?"

Shane frowned when he saw Elliott smiling at Cecily. Cecily had the good grace to glance at each of them and smile. It rubbed him the wrong way. He'd rather she just smiled at him. But that was the way between him and Elliott always vying for the same girl. "I was thinking to sit outside for a while with Elliott's help of course."

Cecily's face brightened. "Now that's a wonderful idea. I'll go and make sure a chair is made comfortable for you." She turned to leave but stopped when Shane spoke.

"Don't go to any trouble. You work hard enough around here as it is." Their gazes locked for a moment before she glanced away.

"No trouble, just a few blankets. It'll give me a chance to clean out your room." Shane wore a grin as he watched her leave until he caught the enchanted expression on Elliott's face. Frowning, he realized Elliott was smitten.

With the help of Poor Boy and Elliott, Shane ended up nicely seated on one of the porch chairs wrapped like a dang mummy. He'd had to fight back many protests. He didn't want to hurt anyone's feelings; they were only trying to make him comfortable. He glanced toward town and saw Lucy coming their way. What a shock it'd been to have her show up. He'd never thought to set eyes on her again. He just wished she would try to get along with Cecily. Somehow, she'd misread his reason for leaving the plantation and the South. How she'd turned an argument between him and his father into some romantic notion, he'd never know. He should've tried to get Elliott alone so he could explain that Lucy was passing. Personally, he was happy for her. If it gave her a leg up in the world, so be it.

He hadn't asked about her travels to Texas. He hadn't asked how she'd gotten money for such fancy clothes. It couldn't have been easy being afraid that she'd be found out. He didn't suspect that others would be so understanding.

Poor Boy scrambled for the front steps yelling something about work he had to do in the barn. Shane watched as he ran as though the very devil himself was chasing him. He raked his fingers through his hair. Maybe Poor Boy was right. Perhaps Lucy *was* the devil in disguise. As she came closer, he could see the pasted smile on her face and a dash of fear in her eyes.

Shane glanced at Elliott, and there wasn't even a flicker of recognition on his face. Elliott had spent time on the plantation but he didn't seem to know Lucy. He was surprised when Elliott stood and nodded his head ever so slowly.

Lucy's eyes widened, and she quickly sought Shane's gaze. She nodded back at Elliott and took a sudden interest in the white trim on the sleeve of her dark blue dress. She stood ever so still as though she was waiting for Elliott to spill her secret.

Elliott cleared his throat and turned towards him. "Aren't you going to introduce me to this lovely lady?" Lucy blinked and gazed from him to Elliott and then back to him.

"Elliott McManus, may I present Lucy O'Connor. She too hails from our fair state of South Carolina. She's been staying here with Cecily and Poor Boy and myself. We don't have a hotel here in town yet." Shane held his breath hoping his lie would hold.

Elliott took Lucy's hand in his and gave her a gentlemanly nod. "It is so very nice to meet you Miss. It is Miss, isn't it?" He smiled as she nodded. "It's a pleasure to meet such a refined Southern woman in the wilds of Texas. I do have to say I am homesick for South Carolina. I miss the niceties of life, but I'm here to make a new life for myself, and I plan on being a great success."

"Why thank you, Mr. McManus," Lucy said.

"Please call me Elliott."

Lucy smiled and tilted her head in a coy manner. "And you may call me Lucy. I too miss a bit of my old life, but I'm finding my new life to be full of wonderful challenges. Isn't that right, Shane? Who would've thought that Shane O'Connor would have ever become the sheriff of any town?"

Shane watched their banter and became decidedly uncomfortable. He had a bad feeling that this would come to a bad end. Why did Lucy have to smile at Elliott? Didn't she know better than to play with fire?

"Please, Elliott, come in I'm sure we can offer you some

refreshment." Lucy waited for Elliott to open the door for her before she entered the house.

Shane wanted to groan out loud. Why couldn't she let well enough alone? She'd best forget about playing lady of the house. He'd talk to her later about it.

"Ready, old friend?" Elliott leaned down and helped Shane to his feet. He nodded at Cecily who held the door open as they made their way inside. "Bedroom or kitchen?"

Cecily said bedroom at the exact same time as Lucy said kitchen. The two women stared at him and not in a friendly way. They both had their arms crossed in front of them and no matter which he decided he was sure to catch the devil from one of them.

"I probably should get some rest." He and Elliott took a few steps towards the bedroom.

"Is that any way to treat a guest? I'm sure Mr. McManus, I mean Elliott, would like some refreshments."

"They can visit just as easily in the bedroom. Shane needs his rest." "Elliott, I do think I should lie down for a bit, but we can talk just as well in there as we can out here. As for refreshments, I would love a cup of coffee." He walked into the bedroom with Elliott's help and sat on the bed.

His old friend looked as though he would burst out laughing at any moment, but he remained silent.

"Don't even say a word."

Elliott helped Shane swing his legs up and got him settled on the bed before he sat in the ladder back chair next to him. "I'd say you had one too many hens in the house. So tell me which one of them is yours?"

"Neither. I have no claim to either of them." Shane bit back a curse when he saw Cecily standing in the doorway with two cups of coffee. He swallowed hard. Damn, she'd probably heard that.

Without looking at him, she handed both cups to Elliott and walked out.

CECILY WISHED she had a place to hide and gather her thoughts. She had believed Shane when he told her she could stay as long as she liked. She should've known the offer was too good to be true. It sounded like he was offering Elliot to pick, between her or Lucy. He didn't need her, he had Lucy and Poor Boy. She was just an extra mouth to feed. Her face heated as she realized how little Shane thought of her. Her soul deflated, and she wished she could run into the woods and keep running, but no one would bother to come after her. Why hadn't she sensed she was a burden?

She took the loaves of bread out of the oven and placed them on the table. She glanced over at Lucy, who was sitting in a chair watching her. It was too much, Lucy knowing how Shane felt. Cecily grabbed her bonnet and her shawl and walked out of the house. She glanced at the woods, wishing to be free but she'd probably end up dead this time. The other times she had run, she hadn't cared whether she lived or died; now she cared. She tied her bonnet on and draped the shawl over her shoulders. Taking a deep breath, she headed toward town.

It was crowded inside the mercantile. What was going on? There must be news of some kind, and she wished she could go in. Instead, she kept walking. It was heartbreaking to know there was a room full of people who would be offended by her presence. Soon enough, she ran out of boardwalk and crossed the street to walk back toward Shane's house. He probably hadn't noticed she was gone. She watched as Cinders and Keegan came out of the mercantile slapping each other on the back. She'd bet anything that both their wives had just given them a child. Normally, the details would've been important to her, but she wasn't included in the good news. Both Shannon and Addy had gone out of their way to be friendly with her, and she wished she was a normal person, able to return their friendship.

She was surprised when Keegan crossed the street and yelled for her to hold up. She turned and waited. Addy sure was a lucky woman, Keegan was a very handsome man.

"Hey, Cecily, it's good to meet you. Addy made me promise to tell you we had a little boy," Keegan said with a great big grin on his face.

She smiled back. "That's wonderful news! I'm so happy for you both. What did you name him?"

Keegan laughed. "Peg insists on helping to name the baby so we're working on her. In fact she wants to name him Shane two. Me, I like the name Ryan and Addie, she hasn't decided yet."

"Shannon told me about Peg and how she likes to name everything. Well whatever you name him, I bet he's a fine baby."

"He sure is. Cinders and Shannon have a little girl they named Olivia. My son doesn't have much hair on his head but little Olivia has a fair amount of red hair, and from what I've heard she has a temper that goes with that red hair."

"Be sure to congratulate them for me. I'm really happy for all of you. I need to get back and make sure Shane isn't trying to tire himself out."

"You might want to tie him to the bed." He laughed and tipped his hat to her. "You take care now, and we'll see you soon."

"Keegan? Thank you for taking the time to tell me, I appreciate it." She drew her shawl tighter around her and headed out of town. It was strange to feel so happy for them while feeling envious at the same time. She hoped they knew how lucky they were. Her eyes teared as she thought of all the babies she wouldn't have.

She quickly dashed away her tears and took a deep breath. It sure had been one of those days full of emotion. She'd better learn to buck up. There certainly wouldn't be time to take a walk every time her feelings got hurt. Sure her life wasn't what she expected, but she could try to make a nice life for herself. She just needed a new plan is all and a backup plan for that plan. Leaving town was probably her best move. All she needed was a bit of traveling money and she could easily save enough in just a few months.

She tried to be serene as she walked up the steps to the house. It would do no good to let on how she felt. She had a feeling that Lucy was the type to jump on another's weakness. She had dinner to get on the table, and she had to figure out the sleeping arrangements. It was more than likely Elliott would be spending the night too.

Walking into the house, she removed her bonnet and then hung it up with her shawl. She went straight to the kitchen but wanted to turn and run when she saw the sour look on Lucy's face.

"Thank goodness you're back." Lucy stood and put her hands on her hips.

"Has something happened?" Cecily's heart beat faster. Had something happened to Shane?

"No, nothing happened. I began to worry about who was going to make dinner. You do know that cooking is part of your duties, don't you?"

Ignoring her, Cecily peeked into the bedroom glad to see that Poor Boy was back. She asked him to fetch her some more wood. She didn't look at either man, and she didn't wait for an answer; it was easier that way. She went to the stove and lifted the lid off the pot of broth picked up a spoon and stirred it, satisfied it appeared to be about ready. The bit of beef she had added that morning had cooked down into small pieces, making the broth nice and rich. After giving it one last stir she replaced the lid.

Lucy walked over to the stove and peeked under the lid. She turned and gazed at Cecily with the same sour look on her face she had before. "You can't seriously be thinking of serving this up as dinner."

"If you're hungry you'll eat it. If not, you won't. It's as simple as that." Poor Boy raced past them and out the front door.

"Perhaps you can make a cobbler or something. You'll shame Shane with that type of food."

Poor Boy came running back in with a load of firewood in his arms and dropped his burden next to the stove. "Here you go." He hurried back into the bedroom. It was good for him to spend time with Shane.

"If you want cobbler, go ahead and make cobbler. It's been a busy day."

Lucy folded her arms in front of her. "Well, maybe if you hadn't decided to take such a long walk you'd have gotten your work done. Work comes first around here. I thought you, of all people, would know that. It's a good thing I came here. Shane deserves better."

"Maybe you should get busy figuring out the sleeping arrangements for tonight."

"What's to figure? You and Poor Boy get the floor. Elliot can take the front room. There are a few comfortable looking chairs there. I get the room of course."

Cecily sighed. "It's fine by me. Just having a roof over my head is enough."

Lucy stared at her and drew her brows together. She shook her head in disgust and walked away mumbling something about trash. Cecily closed her eyes and took a deep calming breath wondering just how long Lucy planned to stay.

Poor Boy came darting out of Shane's bedroom again. "I'll be back in time for dinner," he yelled as he ran out the house.

Cecily laughed. Poor Boy seemed to be a very different person since he'd been here at the house. She noticed he didn't check every corner of the room as he walked through. Then again, perhaps he was too busy.

"What are you laughing about? Lucy asked as she came back into the kitchen, scowling.

"Oh, I don't know, seeing him so excited makes me happy. I know he enjoyed his last job, and he's close with the restaurant's owner, but for some reason he smiles more when he's here." Cecily turned to the stove again, gave the pot a stir, and when she turned back, Lucy had already gone into her room. She put the top on the pot and marched after Lucy.

"I would've thought you'd have gathered your stuff by now."

"I'll just grab a crate and pack my belongings. It won't take long. It's a nice room, don't you think?" Cecily didn't wait for an answer; she went into the kitchen, grabbed an empty crate, and immediately began to fold her clothes and gently place them into it.

"Oh, for Pete's sake everything you do takes forever." Lucy grabbed one of the dresses, folded it into a ball and threw it into the box. Cecily just stared at her dress wondering what could make a person so mean. She finished packing and took her things out of the bedroom. Hopefully, Lucy would need to lie down for a while or something. Maybe Cecily having to leave wasn't such a tragedy after all. She had a feeling that no matter what she did Lucy would thwart her.

Setting the crate on the table Cecily reached in, grabbed the dress and lovingly folded it before it became a wrinkled mess. She held it close to her trying to remember the happiness she'd felt when she first got it.

The front door swung open, and Poor Boy ran back in, smiling from ear to ear.

"What's got you so happy?" Poor Boy's smile was infectious, and before she knew it she was smiling too.

"Shane sent me to the mercantile to conduct some business for him," Poor Boy told her proudly. "We'll have three new mattresses and bedding to go with them. And they are going to be delivered. Isn't it exciting?"

Cecily touched the young boy's arm and rubbed it up and down. "Yes it's very exciting."

"Well us men probably have more to talk about." Poor Boy puffed out his chest. His happiness lightened her heart, and that solved the sleeping dilemma. Dinner was almost ready, and she sliced the bread, glad that she had both butter and preserves to serve with it. She didn't care if Lucy approved of her cooking or not. In fact, if Lucy wanted to cook, Cecily was more than willing to step aside and allow her.

She had just begun to set the bowls around the table when Lucy came out of the bedroom. "You know, you really don't have many clothes. And I find it curious that you don't have any precious mementos. Why aren't you married?" Lucy went behind her and straightened every item she had set on the table.

"It's a long story, and I'd rather not talk about it." Cecily yelled into Shane's room and told the men dinner was ready. She would have liked for Shane to stay in bed, but she knew it would be an argument she'd lose. Everyone sat at the table and waited while Cecily filled their bowls.

"Sure looks good," Shane said as he grabbed up his spoon. His praise warmed her inside.

"Elliott, I'm sorry this is what we are serving. I would

have thought that having a guest would have meant better fare." Lucy's syrupy tone did nothing to ease the sting of her words.

Cecily's appetite fled, and she stared down at her food. She wasn't sure what Lucy was used to eating, but this was common food in Texas. Every time she started to feel good about herself, Lucy was right there to knock her down.

"I'm enjoying it very much. Cecily, you are a fine cook." Elliott smiled when she finally gazed up at him.

"Thank you," she simply said before she bowed her head and stared at her plate again.

"I asked her to make a cobbler, but she refused."

Enough was enough. There was no reason in the world she had to stay here and take Lucy's abuse. She knew she was welcome at Cinders' and Keegan's ranches, and it was time to consider staying with one of them. She shoved away from the table, the abrupt move rattling the dishes. "If you'll excuse me, I need some fresh air."

SHANE'S EYES narrowed as he studied Lucy. She was all smiles as if she had just won some wonderful contest. Damn, why did she have to make trouble wherever she went? He was the one doing her a favor by giving her a place to live. Somehow, she seemed to think she was the lady of the manor. It took a lot of time to travel from South Carolina to Texas; surely she knew the meals were not decadent. He didn't like the game she was playing, not one bit. He needed to talk to Cecily alone, but the house was so crowded he wasn't sure when he'd get a chance.

"I asked her if she was married, and she said she didn't want to talk about it." Lucy offered another smug smile. "She's lying about something."

Elliott cleared his throat. "Well, if she didn't want to talk about it how did she lie to you?"

"It's very simple. If you're honest, you talk about yourself. She doesn't want to talk about it, so she's lying about something." Lucy gave them a decisive nod as though to say she was right and it was the end of the discussion. Shane couldn't help but stare at her. How could a woman who was lying, not just lying but lying big enough to get herself killed call another woman a liar?

"Elliott, give me a hand into my room, will you?" Shane suddenly felt bone tired. He'd thought the house was full with Cecily and Poor Boy, but now it was truly crowded. It wasn't so much it was crowded; most people could deal with a bit of inconvenience, but there were too many different personalities and definitely too much drama. He grunted in pain as he stood and put his good arm over Elliott's shoulder. They proceeded into his room, and by the time he was in bed he wanted to pass out. He nodded his thanks and watched the door close behind Elliot's exit.

He'd have to get in touch with Cinders and let them know he'd be down and out for a bit. After all, Cinders was the one who'd hired him. He wasn't quite sure what to do about Lucy. He'd be willing to help her, but he couldn't marry her, regardless of whatever crazy romantic notions in her head.

Damn his father for being such a hypocrite. Shane had watched more than once from his bedroom window as his father snuck out late at night and headed toward the slave cabins. He'd sworn then and there he would never be like his father. His poor mother. He could see it in her eyes that she knew what his father was up to. She didn't deserve his mistreatment of her. He took a deep breath and let it out ever so slowly. The pain of leaving his boyhood home still ran deep inside him.

Now Elliott, he was a different creature altogether. Shane

frowned and shook his head. He could've sworn Elliott had joined the Confederate Army. Yet he made no mention of having been a soldier. He guessed it didn't matter much. Everyone had something they wanted to keep private. Well, maybe everyone but Cecily; she wasn't hiding anything. Everyone knew her business, she just didn't delve into the details of her torture. Why folks couldn't respect that, he didn't know. It was absurd that people thought she should've killed herself. He wondered what she had been like back in Pennsylvania on that farm of hers. Somehow, he pictured her as carefree and smiling and perhaps she had been at one time.

The knock on the door was light enough he knew it had to be Lucy's. Cecily would rather have him sleep than be bothered. He was so tempted just to close his eyes and pretend he was sleeping but she was his guest. Before he could say come in Lucy was inside his room.

"Just who do you expect to clean the dishes?" Lucy put her hands on her hips and stared at him. He'd never noticed how annoying she could be. She'd always been a bit haughty and in his youth he had laughed it off. Now, he couldn't stand her.

"Well, seeing as this is not a hotel, I guess you could all take turns. It would please me greatly if you did it tonight." It was near impossible keep a straight face as Lucy's jaw dropped open.

"Isn't that Cecily's job?"

"Honestly, Lucy? Whatever happened to the saying many hands make light work? Look, I'm in no condition to be bothered about housework. I expect everyone to work for the roof over their heads. This is Texas, and everyone works for what they want. We don't take kindly to freeloaders."

Lucy gasped and put her hand to her throat. "You, of all people should know I've always worked and gotten nothing in return. Maybe it's my turn to have people work for me. Maybe I would like to sit on the front porch while others provide my every desire."

"Lucy, if I could change the world I would but that's not how things work. There are so many unfair things, and a person has to learn to roll with the punches and get back up again. When I hired Cecily there was just me living here. She did not take a job where she had to cook and clean for three extra people."

Lucy's eyes narrowed, and she glowered at him. "Shane, if she doesn't want the job I'd be glad to take it. But I would expect us to be married. I'll not have others thinking poorly of me."

"Excuse me," Cecily said as she entered the room. "If there's to be a wedding I guess it's time for me to start looking for another place to live. I had hoped to make enough to get to the next town. Is the wedding to be soon?"

Her gaze met his and a jolt went through his body making him feel alive and full of energy. There was something about her, and he didn't want to lose her.

"Cecily, we will be building that farm you wanted. I have no intentions of being married. I have instructed Lucy here to help you around the house. I want everyone to understand I am in charge. And while I'm laid up, I will not put up with any arguing." He directed a hard stare at Lucy. "Sometimes we just all have to learn to get along."

"Fine then I have some things to get done, and I'm sure you need to get more rest, Shane. Oh, by the way, I forgot to tell you both Shannon and Addy had their babies. I talked to Keegan earlier, and he is one proud papa. Shannon and Cinders had a girl with a head full of red hair, and Keegan and Addy have a little boy. Peg is insisting on naming her little brother and guess what name she wants." Cecily's face lit up and humor danced in her eyes. "Shane two, of course."

She laughed as she walked toward the bed and put her hand on his forehead. "No fever, that's a good sign. Now you get some rest."

Shane nodded. He couldn't keep his eyes off her. "You have to admit Shane two is a good name." He sighed. "You're right, I do need to get some rest, so ladies I will talk to you later."

ecily stretched her arms over her head as she sat up. Lucy might have thought she'd stolen the best bed in the house, but the new mattresses were divine. Elliott took one of the front rooms, while she and Poor Boy placed their mattresses before the kitchen stove. Lucy had kept her door closed all night long and it was probably pretty cold in there right now. Luckily for Shane, Cecily knew to leave his door open. How she wished she had some privacy to wash and dress, but she'd muddle through. Things could be and had once been much worse.

Scooping up her blue dress, and draped the dress over the back of one of the wooden chairs and poured a basin of warm water from the pot on the stove. Poor Boy still slept. Quickly, she washed and dressed, praying the whole time no one would walk in. She'd gotten lucky. As soon as she had everything in order, she planned to make pancakes. For some reason Shane had a whole bunch of honey in the root cellar. She'd have to ask him about that sometime. She also put coffee on to boil and sliced the pork into strips of bacon.

When the coffee was done, she poured a cup and carried

it in to Shane. It was no surprise he was awake, given the pain he was in. His weary eyes smiled at her, and he seemed pleased she brought him coffee.

"Good morning, Shane. Feeling any better today?" she asked as she set the cup down on the table next to the bed. "I'll have breakfast ready in no time at all. I'll bring it into you, I don't want you getting out of bed this morning."

The lines around Shane's eyes crinkled as he smiled. "When did you turn into my mother?"

Cecily's mouth dropped open as she shook her head. "I guess when you got shot."

"Have I thanked you for all your help? If not, I am truly grateful. I know things have been a bit hectic around here, but I'm hoping things get back to normal soon."

"Oh, and what exactly is normal?"

Shane laughed. "To tell you the truth I really don't know. I do have a cow and some chickens coming today. I had Poor Boy buy them when he ordered the mattresses. Will you need help with that?"

She leaned over, gently lifted his shoulders and moved his pillow so he was in a more upright position. Handing him his coffee she smiled. Her smile warmed him like nothing else ever had. "Poor Boy promised to make a chicken coop for me. I don't think I've ever come across a cow that I can't handle. Of course, I don't know much about Texas cows but the ones from Pennsylvania are friendly enough."

Shane continued to chuckle. "I guess I just assumed all cows were alike, but be careful just the same. If anything, they're probably more ornery here in Texas."

His high spirits gladdened her heart. So far, she'd had a great start to her day. The only thing she dreaded was Lucy waking up. It was all bound to be downhill from there and then some. Hopefully, the cows and chickens would arrive first thing giving her an excuse to be out of the house and away from that woman.

"Enjoy your coffee, I'll be back in a bit with your breakfast." She turned, and when she got to the door she turned again. "Why do you have so much honey?"

"Keegan has the best honey around, and Cinders gave me the tip to get some while I could. Have you tasted it yet?"

"No, but it sounds intriguing."

"We'll talk after you taste it."

She hastened from the room back to the kitchen.

Poor Boy was up and heading out the front door. He must've heard her come out of Shane's room, and he paused and looked over his shoulder at her. "I'm gonna check on Jester. Looking forward to the honey." He grinned and slipped out the door.

She'd have to remember not to say anything she didn't want others to hear. She quickly made the batter, put the bacon on to fry, and set the table. Next, she went down to the root cellar to grab some of that delicious honey. She couldn't help herself. Before going back up the steps she put her finger into the honey and popped her finger into her mouth. Shane hadn't exaggerated one bit, the honey was heavenly.

The overhead door closed with a sudden thud, sending her into total darkness. Puzzled, she gingerly climbed the stairs and pushed up on the door. To her consternation, it didn't budge. There was only one lock on the door and that was on the inside of the root cellar. So why couldn't she get it open? She called out, but no one answered. Her heart beat faster as she tried to remember if she had seen lamps and matches. Closing her eyes, she tried to imagine where everything was kept, and to her delight she did remember oil lamps in the far right corner. She took a deep breath. Now if they were filled she might be set.

Slowly, she set the jar of honey on the top step and

cautiously made her way down the stairs in the darkness. She shuffled her feet on the ground so as not to trip on anything until she finally made it to the corner. The stone wall was cold against her palm as she felt around until she brushed against a lamp. She hoped her eyes would adjust, but it was just so pitch black she still couldn't see. Luckily, next to the lamps she encountered matches.

She sighed in relief and felt the lamp with her fingers to see exactly how this one worked. Thankfully it was a simple straight up-and-down glass one. She got it lit and found her way back to the stairs. She stopped and listened, wondering why nobody had come when she called. All was silent. Frowning, she walked back up the steps and tried once more to push open the door. To her consternation it still wouldn't move. What in the world? She sat on the steps and decided to wait. Poor Boy would be back soon enough.

She held the lamp up and looked around the root cellar from where she sat. She had a feeling that there was another entrance hidden somewhere, but for the life of her she couldn't spot it. She finally heard footsteps, and she knocked on the door calling out to whoever it was. She followed the footsteps as they came to the door and walked away again. She'd bet that was Lucy. Why was that woman giving her so much trouble?

She heard Poor Boy's voice and this time she pounded as hard as she could while calling out to him. Relief rushed through her as the door lifted up. Poor Boy stared at her with the oddest expression on his face.

"What you doing down there?" he asked. He took the lamp from her and offered her his hand to guide her up the steps.

After closing the door, she looked around to see what had kept her from opening the door. There, next to the opening sat the water tub filled with heavy bags of flour, beans, coffee, and a barrel of pickles. It was no wonder she wasn't able to lift the door. Why? Why would Lucy go to so much trouble to make her angry? Was she trying to cause trouble hoping Shane would ask her to leave? It was a mean spiteful thing to do, but she wasn't going to mention a word of it to Shane. He didn't need anymore headaches.

"I was getting the honey and I got locked in, but I'm fine now. I'd best get on with making the pancakes. I bet everyone is hungry." She ignored Poor Boy's puzzled gaze as she walked by him and went into the kitchen. She also ignored Lucy who was sitting at the kitchen table drinking coffee with the sugar bowl right in front of her. How she wanted to smack the gloating smile off her face, but it just might make Lucy angrier if she ignored her. She was obviously waiting for some type of reaction. Too bad she was going to be disappointed. Surprisingly, someone had cooked the bacon and taken it off the stove.

"Good morning, ladies. It looks to be a fine day outside." Elliott smiled at them both.

"Poor Boy, could you get Elliott a cup of coffee while I get these pancakes made?"

Poor Boy smiled, as always, eager to help, and before she knew it, she had everything cooked and ready to go. She made up a tray for Shane. Lucy arched an eyebrow as she stared her down, but Cecily was determined not to be intimidated by this mean-spirited woman. Before serving the rest of them, she took the tray into Shane's room.

"Here you go," she said to Shane as she placed the tray on his lap. "Can I bring you more coffee?"

"Is something going on I should know about? I heard you knocking and yelling from the root cellar. I called for someone to help you as I couldn't get up myself."

"Nothing for you to be worried about. I'll send Poor Boy

in with more coffee." She gave him a quick smile and left the room. Not much got past him.

"It's about time—"

"Lucy, I really don't want to hear it. The food is right there, and you could've helped yourself or at the very least served Elliott and Poor Boy some breakfast. I'm not sure how you got the impression that we have an employer servant relationship, but we don't. My boss is Shane, and only Shane. I know he explained to you that this is a working farm. Which means if you want to eat, you earn your food. Now, there are plenty of ways for you to do that, such as cooking, cleaning, washing clothes, or helping to tend the animals. We're expecting a cow and some chickens today. You could help with those if you'd like." She turned away as Lucy gasped. Cecily grabbed a plate, filled it and handed it to Elliott. She did the same for Poor Boy and finally for herself. Poor Boy's eyes were big and round as he watched Cecily sit at the table without offering Lucy anything to eat.

Cecily shrugged her right shoulder and promptly ignored Lucy. It surprised her how long it took for Lucy to actually get up and get her own breakfast. Well that was too bad. Boundaries needed to be set and they needed to be set now. As soon as Cecily was done she went into Shane's room with coffee pot in hand.

He still had dark shadows under his eyes but his color was looking better. His hair was practically standing on end, and she was surprised she hadn't noticed it before. She crossed the room and filled his cup of coffee. "I forgot to send Poor Boy in to pour you more."

"Breakfast was good, thank you," he said as he handed her the tray.

He stared at her as though he could read her mind, and it made her decidedly uncomfortable. If he only knew how attractive he was to her. Her face heated. "I'm glad you liked it. And you were right. Keegan's honey is amazing. I've never tasted better. Let me put these things in the kitchen, and I'll be right back to check your wound and make sure your fever is still gone."

"Thank you for taking care of me. I can't remember a time in recent years when someone has looked out for me like you have. Make a list of what you'd like to plant, and I'll send Poor Boy to buy the seeds. I'll find someone to till the garden and get it ready for planting."

"You don't need to hire anyone to do anything. I can handle it all by myself. I did want to ask you something but think it over before you say yes. What about putting a small crop in? We'll have to ask around and see what grows in the Texas soil. I plan to make the garden big enough to feed us through the winter with extra to sell. And if we have a crop that people want we can sell that to. I'm good at making soap and candles, so I bet I can sell those too."

"You sure are amazing." Shane smiled at her.

"Let me put these dishes away, and I'll be right back." She couldn't help but smile back at him. She hoped he saw her as an asset to his household. She turned toward the door and brushed past Lucy who stood just outside the door listening to their conversation.

"I'll check Shane for fever, and when you bring the water in I'll wipe him down with a cool cloth. It sounds to me like you'll be too busy to take care of Shane." Lucy gave Cecily a sarcastic smile and then turned that smile into one of sunshine as she entered Shane's room.

There was no predicting that woman. One minute she refused to help with Shane's care, and the next minute she insisted on being the caretaker. Whatever was to her advantage. She didn't seem to have a genuine bone in her body. Cecily made fast work of the dishes and filled the basin with cool water. Grabbing a clean cloth, she walked into Shane's room and handed the basin to Lucy. Giving Shane a quick smile she hurried from the room not wanting to see Lucy's breasts pouring over the top of her fancy dress. She'd learn soon enough that a dress like that wasn't practical.

The sound of a wagon approaching and the mooing of the cow made Cecily laugh. She snatched her bonnet from the peg, put it on, and then grabbed her shawl. She had better things to do than think about Lucy. Happily, she left the house.

———

SHANE GRITTED his teeth and turned his gaze away from Lucy and her overflowing cleavage. He knew what she was all about, and he had no intention of playing her game. She didn't wring out the cloth and soon enough he was soaked as was the bedding beneath him. It was more than likely she had never tended to another person in her life. He closed his eyes and when she began to stroke his hair with her hand, he quick as lightning grabbed her wrist and pulled it away from his head. He heard her gasp, but quite frankly he didn't care.

"It's bad enough that you're in here without you touching my hair. I know it hurts you to hear it, but there is nothing between us. I'm sorry, Lucy, but you have to set your sights on some other man." He expected to see pain on her face, but instead he saw hatred and the need for revenge. It threw him that she could be so changeable. He had a sudden gut feeling she could be dangerous if she wanted to be.

She set the basin and the cloth on the table next to the bed, stood, and walked out of the room without looking at him. Shane sighed and frowned. He hadn't a clue how to deal with her.

He could hear Cecily's light laughter outside and longed to be out there with her. He shook his head, and his heart pinged. Cecily didn't want a man in her life, and he wasn't going to try to change her mind. She'd already suffered more than most women had at the hands of men. Still it would've been nice to see the look of joy on her face instead of picturing it. He glanced at the door when he heard someone approach.

Upon stepping inside, Elliott laughed. "Did they give you a bath and forget to give you a towel?"

"This is Lucy's way of keeping my skin cool. Plus, she's mad at me. Be a good friend and find a towel for me please."

"I'll even do one better, I'll find you something dry to wear." Elliott left the room and quickly returned with the towel, clean sheets. He rifled through a few drawers and grabbed clean clothes. He helped Shane take off his wet clothes, sat him on the wooden chair and threw him a towel. As soon as Shane was dry Elliott handed him the clothes. "Need some help?"

Shane shook his head. "Thanks but I can take it from here." He heard some arguing going on outside and stood. He started to sway a bit, but Elliott came to his side and wrapped his arm around his waist.

"I can put the dry sheets on your bed."

"No, that's fine, just leave them. Help me outside will you? I want to see what the shouting is all about." Shane put his good arm around Elliott's shoulder and together they made their way to the front porch. Perspiration broke out on Shane's brow as he sat back down.

Lucy was squawking, Cecily had her arms crossed in front of her looking as though she wanted to slap Lucy, and Poor Boy stared at the ground. Mr. Hopkins, a nearby rancher, looked perplexed as he glanced from one woman to the other. He spotted Shane and a look of relief spread over his face.

"Maybe we should ask the owner of the property," Mr. Hopkins said. Both women turned around and stared.

"What's going on out here?"

Lucy was first by his side. "I told you she was trouble. She thinks she's in charge around here."

Cecily walked to the porch and gave him a nod as did Mr. Hopkins.

"So what's the problem?" Shane asked with his attention on Mr. Hopkins.

"Shane, I brought you a milk cow not a steer to be butchered for meat. The same with the laying hens. You'll need the hens for eggs. There's also a rooster which you will need." He glared at Lucy. "Not for eating. I'm not sure, Shane. I thought you were going to build a farm. If you need chickens for food or a steer to butcher I have those too. Eventually you'll have enough chickens for food too but not to start."

"Mr. Hopkins we are building that farm and you brought out exactly what I needed. I guess there's been a little misunderstanding between the women. Cecily and I are planning a farm and I suppose I didn't let Lucy know any of the details. I'm sorry about the argument."

The tension seemed to leave Mr. Hopkins body as his shoulders relaxed. "Well as long as we're on the same page everything's fine. I have some pigs that are almost weaned if you're interested."

"Of course we are," Cecily said excitedly as she turned to Shane for confirmation.

"We most assuredly are." A pleasant tenderness filled him, and a grin spread across his face. Cecily's excitement was contagious.

Lucy crossed her arms across her chest and tapped her toe. "What about food? We can't eat what she cooks." She nodded her head toward Cecily.

Elliott had kept quiet the whole time, but now he stepped forward. "Cecily is a fine cook. A lot of us have been through hard times lately, and I know I'm grateful to have food in my stomach and a roof over my head."

Lucy peered at them one by one and then shrugged her shoulders. "I was just hoping for something different than watery soup. I thought we'd all appreciate some chicken or steak for a change."

Shane shook his head and grinned. "You've only been here for a short time, Lucy. In fact, we had chicken a few days ago. This is our dream, Cecily's and mine, to build a farm. I'm sorry, Lucy, but you have no say in it."

Elliott chuckled, Mr. Hopkins nodded in satisfaction, and Lucy clenched her teeth. The fact that Cecily didn't gloat over him taking her side warmed his heart.

"I made a chicken coop and everything, Shane! I bought everything you said and look." Poor Boy told him excitedly.

Shane looked farther out into the yard, and to his surprise there sat a finely constructed chicken coop. His gaze met Cecily's and she was full of pride. "You did a mighty fine job, Poor Boy. It's better than anything I could've made. I'm very proud of you." Poor Boy turned a bright shade of red, and he grinned from ear to ear.

Cecily touched Poor Boy on the arm. "Come on, let's get those chickens into the coop."

Shane stood and watched as Cecily, Poor Boy and Mr. Hopkins all gathered the chickens and put them into the new construction. His heart filled with happiness as he observed the joy on Cecily's face. Who could have known that chickens could make a woman so happy? As soon as they were done Mr. Hopkins led Cecily to the back of his wagon, where the brown cow was tied. Feeling a bit woozy, Shane sat down on one of the porch chairs and watched. Cecily checked out the cow from top to bottom and from nose to tail. She checked its legs looked at its teeth and ran her hands over its back.

She laughed at something Mr. Hopkins said and nodded. Mr. Hopkins untied the rope from his wagon and handed it to Cecily. He gave Shane a wave and he nodded to Cecily before he got into his wagon and drove away.

Cecily led the cow to the porch. "She looks to be a good one. What do you think?"

Seeing her eyes lit with such pleasure warmed his heart. He would've agreed with her even if the cow was without udders. "She looks mighty fine to me." Her happiness became his and he found himself smiling right back at her.

"Poor Boy, come on let's find a place in the barn for Bessie."

Lucy frowned and put her hand on Shane's shoulder. "You're going to let her name your cow?" Shane tilted his head up and narrowed his eyes as he stared at Lucy.

"I don't see that it's any of your business." His voice was harsher than he had intended but he'd had enough of Lucy's interference.

"Lucy, why don't you and I take a stroll into town?" Elliott asked. "I have some business I need to attend to."

Lucy gave him a flirtatious smile and nodded her head. "Why, thank you, Elliott, I would love the distraction and the pleasure of your company, of course."

Shane gave Elliott a nod of thanks and sat back in the chair relieved. He needed to get himself well and soon. The town needed him and he needed to get the heck out of the house.

"Let me grab my hat and we can be on our way." Shane and Elliott watched Lucy go back into the house.

"What type of business do you have in town?"

"I need to stop at the bank, and I would like to get a feel of the town. My wandering days are over. I want to settle down. Do you have a claim on Lucy?"

Shane shook his head. "We're just childhood friends."

Lucy smiled at them both as she came through the door with her elegant lace-trimmed hat placed on her head. He had to admit she looked every inch the fine lady.

"You two have a good time now. Don't forget to find out all the gossip and see if anyone has been taking time to look after the town."

"I wouldn't worry about the town," Elliott said. "I think if they needed you, they would have sent somebody out to tell you."

Shane nodded. "I bet you're right about that."

Elliott offered Lucy his arm, and she slid her hand into the crook of his elbow, tilting her head up and smiling at him. Shane just hoped she told Elliott the truth before things went much further. Secrets had a way of coming out at the worst times, and Lucy's secret could be deadly. He wasn't one of those who thought that freeing the slaves was enough. People didn't change overnight. Most of those who fought to free the slaves didn't want them as their friends. Doors would slam in Lucy's face, and she'd be lucky if she wasn't harmed in some way. He'd do his best to protect her. He'd have to have a talk with her where Elliott was concerned.

The laughter coming from the barn lifted his spirits. Somehow, Cecily had gotten under his skin and he wasn't sure it was a good thing. In fact, the more he thought about it, it wasn't a good thing at all. She'd never allow another man to touch her. She'd been through so much. He admired her good nature, her generosity of heart, and her strength. It was better to be friends than nothing at all, but he couldn't help the yearning he felt for her. He wanted to be the one to make her feel safe. He wanted to hold her in his arms, and he wanted her to hold him too.

He'd never experienced a great love or passion for a woman before. He had just never found the right woman until now. It was just his luck she was the wrong woman. She didn't want a husband. His heart squeezed wondering if he would actually be able to live with her, wanting her, loving her, and not being able to have her. If John Hardy hadn't already been dead, he'd kill him. A long, painful death was what he'd deserved. Shane pushed himself up to a standing position, wishing he was able to make it to the barn, but in his condition his room would have to do.

Slowly, step by painful step, he walked to his room. Another few days, and he'd be back at work, he was certain of it. He went to sit on the bed, but remembered it was wet, so he sat on the chair instead. Lost in thought, he didn't hear Cecily come into the room until she touched his arm.

"What happened to your bed?"

"Lucy is what happened. She was cooling me off." He tried to keep from smiling, but it wasn't working.

Her lips twitched as her eyes filled with merriment. "Looks to me like she was trying to drown you. Let me strip off the sheets, and then I'll put the new ones on for you." The chair was so close to the bed that every move she made was almost unbearable for him. He wanted to touch her graceful neck and kiss her right behind her ear while cupping her cheek with his other hand. Perhaps she would laugh and turn her head so he could plant a kiss on her delectable rosy lips.

Her arms laden with the wet sheets, she tried to walk in front of the chair and suddenly she lost her footing. She landed on his lap with the wet sheets between them. Immediately she tried to stand up but he couldn't help himself and he put his good arm around her. He held her loosely not wanting her to panic.

"Shane, you're getting us both soaked," she told him matter-of-factly, but making no attempt to move.

"Honey, with you around it's best I'm cooled off. I can't seem to take my eyes off you, and I don't know how to approach you. I don't want to frighten you, I don't want to cheapen you. I don't want you to think it's part of your job, and I don't want you to do anything you don't want to. I'm content to just watch you and enjoy your company." He waited for her to scramble off his lap, but she still made no attempt to move.

Her eyes were wide, and she gazed into his as though she was trying to read his mind. It was as if she was trying to gauge the truthfulness of the statement. An array of emotions crossed her face. She looked surprised then happy then doubtful and puzzled, and finally wary. "I don't know what to say. You are a good man, Shane O'Connor, and it would only dishonor your name to have mine attached to it. I wish I had met you before I was given to Long Nose. Lord knows, I'd be the happiest woman on earth to hear your words, but that's not how things happened. I'm not considered good enough for you, and it would break my heart if someone thought the lesser of you because of me. I like sitting here with you like this, even if we are getting wet. You make me feel special, but you have your whole life ahead of you and someone like Lucy would be a better choice for you." Her voice wobbled as tears filled her eyes. She gave him a sad smile and pushed to her feet taking the wet sheets with her as she walked out of the room.

His heart squeezed in pain and then it squeezed again even more painfully. She was right. Oh, not about the Lucy part, but maybe about how others would see her. He wasn't about to accept her answer, though. His heart wouldn't allow it, and he didn't have the strength to turn his back on her. It would never be enough just having her work for him, but for now he'd have to take only what she offered.

CHAPTER SIX

*I*t'd been two days since Shane had said such joyous but anguish-filled words to her. Part of her wanted to scream to the world that she loved Shane O'Connor, and part of her wanted to shrivel in shame. She held his words locked in her heart afraid to take them out and examine them. She knew if she started to cry or feel sorry for herself she'd be lost. Her strength had gotten her through the worst of times, and she needed to hold onto it now.

Her only solitude had been the garden, the chickens, the cow, and Poor Boy. She needed to go down into the root cellar again. So far she'd only gone down there when either Shane or Poor Boy were in the kitchen. Right now neither were around but as far she knew both Lucy and Elliott had gone into town again. Taking a deep breath, she quickly opened the door in the floor and hurried down the steps. She grabbed what she needed for venison stew and turned to go up the steps again. She paused as she felt a slight breeze against her skin. There *was* another entrance she just needed to find it when she had time.

She put the meat on the table to cut it into smaller pieces.

Suddenly, loud cursing came from Shane's room. What on earth? She wiped her hands and walked toward his room. He appeared in the doorway clean-shaven looking more handsome than she'd ever seen him.

"You shouldn't be up and about. You'll only hurt yourself."

Shane gave her a cocky smile and folded his arms across his broad chest. "Darlin', the town needs me. I am the sheriff, you know. Doesn't do no good for me to just sit around in bed." She opened her mouth but he raised his hand to stop her. "Don't bother, I'm going anyway."

She'd seen that obstinate expression on his face before. Arguing would do no good. She nodded and tilted her head staring at him. "Just be careful, please?"

He came and stood right in front of her then cupped her shoulders and gave them a slight squeeze. "Always." Then he walked to the front door, grabbed his gun belt and hat, and gave her one last glance before he disappeared through the door.

It was nice to see him well enough to be up and around, but somehow she liked it better when he was at home with her. He'd given her the first sense of peace she'd felt since the War Between the States started. Oh Lord, a lot had happened in her life since the start of the awful war. She was no longer the naïve, happy girl she had once been. Instead, she was a weary woman with a questionable future, just trying to make a life for herself.

She cut the meat and vegetables into pieces and made her stew. The wash needed to be done, and just like every other day when there was work to be done, Lucy was nowhere to be found. Elliott was often absent too. What part of everyone had to work didn't they understand? It was obvious they still thought themselves to be guests, while she and Poor Boy were the servants.

Perhaps it was better that way. She was certain she'd end

up slapping Lucy. It was just about all she could do to keep a civil tongue while being insulted by that woman.

Where they went and what they did for most the day, she didn't know, and frankly, she didn't care. She had more important things to consider. She needed to purge her mind of all thoughts of Shane. She had too many romantic ideas in her head, and it would do no good. Things like his fresh soap and water scent, his wonderfully clean-shaven face, and his beautiful heart-stopping smile. When he'd touched her shoulders, she'd felt a huge spark between them.

It bewildered her; she'd never felt anything quite like it before. She was so aware of him it scared her. She'd never had feelings like this for her fiancé, God rest his soul. Placing her hand over her heart, she walked to the front window and smiled at all the progress they'd made in such short time. It dawned on her she hadn't been running around checking the windows. Shane made her feel safe and it was a feeling she never imagined she'd ever have again.

The smile on her face as she walked back to the kitchen surprised her. She made quick work of finishing the stew and put it on the stove to cook. She couldn't get the image of Shane's smile out of her mind, and she felt like she was glowing from the inside out. When she found herself humming, she instantly stopped. He wasn't for her. He deserved an untainted woman, one who was fit to be the wife of the town sheriff. One whom he could be proud of and, of course, he needed a wife the town would embrace. Unfortunately, she didn't meet any of the qualifications.

A wave of sadness poured over her almost knocking her to her knees. It would hurt so much if she left. She paced the length of the kitchen and stopped. It would also be torture to be around him, loving him, knowing she had no chance of ever winning his love. Taking hold of a bucket, she filled it with water, then picked up a stiff brush and got down on her hands and knees to scrub the floor.

She'd been at it for some time before she heard the door open. "Take off your shoes. I'm cleaning the floors," she called out. She shook her head in dismay as she heard footsteps coming toward her. Whoever was coming still had their shoes on. Looking up she wasn't surprised to see Lucy standing there glaring at her.

"Oh my, there's nothing worse than being on your hands and knees all day scrubbing floors." Lucy looked down at her and shook her head.

"There's another brush if you'd like to help me." Cecily didn't even look up as she continued cleaning the floor.

Lucy was so quiet Cecily finally raised her head and peered at her. "Was there something you wanted?"

"Your back is bleeding. Come on let me take a look at it."

Was this Lucy actually being nice? "Thank you, but I'm sure it's fine."

"Either I can tend to it or I can go get Shane. Which would you rather I do?" Lucy put her hands on her hips and raised her eyebrows.

Cecily had felt the pain but decided to ride it through and get the floors done. It had seemed like a good idea at the time, but it was clearly a big mistake. "Thanks for telling me, but I think I can tend to it myself." She shifted to stand and fiery pain spread across her back between her shoulders and down to her waist. She groaned and sank back to the floor.

"Come on, we might as well get it over with. Attending to you is not my idea of fun. Let's go into my room, shall we? " Cecily bit the inside of her mouth to keep herself from saying something caustic as she stood. Lucy's *shall we* wasn't a question; it was a command. Cecily followed Lucy into the bedroom and began to unbutton her dress. She let it slide down to her waist and stood there with her back facing Lucy.

"The chemise, it has to come off too. I'll go get a basin of cool water and some clean cloths." Cecily lifted her chemise over her head. As she studied it, she was surprised to see so much blood staining it. She should probably skip Lucy's ministrations and just go to see the doctor. She started to pull the chemise back over her head when Lucy walked into the room. The gasps she heard seemed to echo throughout the house. Shamed, Cecily hung her head and closed her eyes willing herself not to cry.

"Sakes alive, who whipped you? From the look of your back it was more than one whipping too. The marks on top aren't all that old."

Cecily willed herself to remain silent in fear that anything said would be all over the town by the end of the day. "I really should get to the doctor. I appreciate your help, Lucy, but Doc has dealt with these before, and I'm sure he'll fix me up again."

"If that's what you want, I'll go get the doctor. You stay here, lie down on my bed and rest. I'll be right back."

Cecily nodded and waited until she heard Lucy leave before she allowed her tears to fall. Truth be told, her back was in excruciating pain. Humiliation swept through her. Lucy had seen, and she would probably tell. Even if she did move to a different town, how would she explain the marks on her back? Sure she could invent a cruel, dead husband but she was tired of lies. They just wore her out as they went against her very nature.

Try as she might, she couldn't stem the tears in her soul, it was filled with torment. The door opened and closed and she sighed in relief hoping the doc would be quick.

"Cecily, what's going on? I saw…"

Oh, dear Lord, no. When she heard Shane's voice, she

wished she could run and hide but she didn't have the will inside her anymore. The bed dipped as Shane sat at the edge next to her. At any other time, she would have scrambled to cover herself, but it didn't seem to matter anymore.

"Oh honey, this looks pretty bad. Why didn't you tell me? You must be in agony, yet you kept on working."

"I—I didn't want to give you an excuse to throw me out. Besides, I'm tough, I've had to be. The doc will fix me up right as rain, and I'll get the floor finished today. I'm just so embarrassed I never wanted anyone to see me like this." She winced at how wobbly her voice was.

"Cecily, you don't have to worry I will not throw you out. I offered you a home not temporary housing. Oh, how you must've suffered at the hands of Long Nose. You're an incredibly strong woman to have survived all this. I just don't understand how one person could do this to another."

The tears continued to fall, and she couldn't get them to stop. "He destroyed my life and my dreams. I so wanted to be a wife and a mother, and to help my husband build his dream whether it was a ranch or a farm. I had hoped to find a fine man to love and one that would eventually love me back. I wish I was skilled at something. Shannon sews so beautifully, she could open her own shop, Addy has many skills of her own. Both of those women could make it on their own. Even Edith has her mercantile."

"Being a wife and a mother is a fine dream, and you'd be an asset to any man you marry. Honey, you have plenty of skills. Didn't you tell me not to buy things at the store because you could make many of them? Making butter and candles and soap, being able to start a farm, those are all skills."

She nodded stiffly. His words were meant as words of comfort; instead they were an arrow to her heart. There was no man who wanted her and her skills were the skills of a wife and homemaker.

"The doc is here. I'll leave you two alone." He got off the bed and greeted the doc. She heard the doctor come in and shut the door behind him.

"I thought I told you to take it easy, young lady. You've broken open a few of the wounds. Are you in pain?"

She nodded and cried out as he cleaned her wounds. Clutching the sheets in her hands she tried to lie as still as possible. After what seemed a long time, he was done.

"I'm not going to bandage these right now. I want you to stay in bed on your stomach and let the air get to your back. In other words, I don't want you covering your back. I'll return in time for supper to bandage you up. I don't want you getting out of bed, and I know for fact that dinner's already on the stove, and I must say it smells mighty good."

There was a light knock at the door.

The doc yelled out, "Come in."

The door slowly swung open, and Shane stood in the doorway hesitantly before he took a step into the room. "So what's the verdict, Doc?" Lying on her stomach she had her head turned toward the door. Even through her pain-induced haze he was still the handsomest man she'd ever seen.

"She'll live if that's what you're asking. But you need to make a few changes around here. Cecily is to lie in bed on her stomach with her back exposed to help with the healing. She's doing too much around here. I want her to have this room to herself. I'll be back in time for dinner to check on her. You're going to have to make other arrangements as far as the cooking and cleaning go. This little gal needs time to heal."

Shane met her gaze and gave her a sympathetic smile. "We'll do whatever it takes to keep Cecily comfortable so she can get better. Don't worry about the chores. We have plenty of people here to take care of things." For a brief moment, she forgot her pain as the amusement of his statement hit her. Sure, there were plenty of people, but who was going to take care of things?

The doc gave her some laudanum, and she was in a fog as he instructed Shane on the dosage. She watched them walk out the door and heard it gently close before her body totally relaxed enough for her to sleep.

Confusion overcame her as she opened her eyes. What time is it? There were no windows in the room and she hadn't a clue. Searing pain ripped through her when she tried to move. Just as she was about to call out to see who was home she heard voices.

"She has to go," Lucy insisted. "Shane, I don't think you realize the impact she is having on your integrity. Why I wouldn't be a bit surprised if they were thinking of getting a new sheriff. One that does not have a woman dirtied by some Indians. Anyway I thought you were supposed to kill yourself before you allowed yourself to be captured. If you won't think of your own reputation, think of mine. No decent person in this town will want to associate with you. There must be some other place she can go. You know she's just taking advantage of your kindness."

A lump formed in Cecily's throat as fear and resentment clutched her heart. She'd known all along that it wasn't right for her to be living with the sheriff. Perception was everything in a small town, and she was doing him an injustice by staying. Lucy was a mean, spiteful woman, but she did have a point.

"She's not going anywhere," Shane said, his voice coming out in an angry hiss. "It wasn't her fault what happened. Good gravy, where did you get the idea that it was better to be dead than survive? Do you know how hard it is to survive something like that? We should all be admiring her courage instead of running her down. She is just my housekeeper and my partner on my farm, but that's it. I don't want to hear another word about it."

Cecily couldn't breathe. She could've sworn Shane had feelings for her. Now, he made it sound as though they weren't even friends, and that cut deep. It was as though something had died inside of her at that moment, and she realized it was hope. Her hope had died. She'd stupidly thought she might have a normal life after all. Of course, Shane would never marry her but she thought that they were close friends; apparently not. Her heart felt heavy and her soul, was weary, so weary. She prayed often asking why her, but she never got an answer. The worst part was, she couldn't leave, not with her back in such bad condition.

Lucy and Shane were still talking but their voices had turned into soft murmurs. She really didn't need to hear anymore, she'd heard the most important thing. Where would she go? What would she do? She was too tired and in too much pain to give it serious thought. But soon she'd have to figure something out.

The door opened, and Shane entered the room. She hadn't noticed before but as broad as he was he made the room feel much smaller. A few hours ago his presence would have given her comfort, but now it was incredibly awkward.

Shane sat down in the chair next to the bed and reached out to touch her shoulder. A shiver went through her, and she wanted to cry. She'd never find another man like Shane, and she was afraid that any man that might happen to want her would never measure up to him.

"How are you doing? How bad is the pain?" he asked in a gentle manner. He stroked her bare shoulder with his large work-worn hand. "I'm sorry you suffered so much. I feel as though this is my fault. If I had known that John Hardy gave you to Long Nose sooner I could've prevented much of what happened to you."

"You didn't know, plain and simple. It's not your fault, and I don't want you blaming yourself. It's done and it's over. The consequences will be lifelong for me, but I couldn't kill myself. I had a couple of chances to throw myself over a cliff, but I kept thinking any day maybe help would come. I'm scared, sometimes I'm afraid of my own shadow, and I bring disgrace to anyone who tries to be a friend."

"Darlin', that's just not true. You have not disgraced me, and I consider you my friend. As for your scars, they won't matter to the right man, and truthfully I think everyone's afraid of their own shadow at one time or another." He stroked her cheek with the back of his hand and moved his hand over her hair. Sometimes, there ain't no way to change the way things are or the way things are going to be."

His sympathetic smile brought more tears to her eyes. If only he was telling the truth, but unfortunately he wasn't. She would be damned if she left and damned if she stayed. For now, she'd heal and carefully plan her future. She looked into his eyes, and if she hadn't heard his conversation with Lucy, she would've thought she saw love shining through them.

"Is Lucy mad I took her bed?"

"This is a working farm, and we all do what we have to. She'll be fine. The doctor should be back anytime now."

"I slept that long?"

"You sure did, darlin'. The sleep is good. It helps the body heal, and you don't feel the pain when you're sleeping."

His hand stroking her hair had a calming effect, and it made her feel safe. It was one of those moments in time she wished would never end. Even though he was just a friend, his touch filled her heart. He stood and kissed the side of her forehead.

"I'd best get out there and make sure dinner doesn't burn. I haven't seen Elliot all day. It's kind of strange if you ask me, but it's not my business. Poor Boy asked if he could come in after dinner and read you a story."

Her eyes widened. "I didn't know he knew how to read. I guess I just assumed he couldn't, that no one ever taught him. I should know better than to judge a person by appearances. Please tell him I'd be delighted to have him visit me. I hope I'm not making any trouble for you. I don't want to be a burden."

"You're not a burden darlin'. Don't you worry about it." Shane walked to the door and turned just enough so he could see her. "You get some rest. The doc will be here soon." He turned back and walked out the door quietly closing it behind him.

SHANE RAN his fingers through his hair as he stood next to the door he had just closed. How could he explain to her that the past was the past and life held so much for her? Of course, it was hard with everything she'd been through and people in their judgmental ways made sure she'd never forget. Maybe she just needed time. Maybe she just needed to know she was safe. He hoped his talk with Lucy made her forget her nonsense about his reputation. He hated lying but he was willing to do anything to protect Cecily.

"Shane, did you ask her? Did she say yes?" The eagerness on Poor Boy's face did his heart good. Poor Boy shifted from one leg to the other waiting for a response.

"I sure did, and she said yes she'd be delighted."

"She said delighted? Are you sure?" Shane put his hand on the boy's shoulder and laughed.

"Yes Cecily did say that."

Lucy turned from the stove and glared at both of them. "I really could use some help here. You all have been too busy playing nursemaid to that woman."

Poor Boy crossed his arms in front of him and returned Lucy's glare. "Her name is Cecily and she is the finest lady I know. She deserves kindness and all things good."

Shane nodded in agreement. He'd never seen Poor Boy so worked up. Usually, he was pretty easy-going and eager to please. Shane was about to add his thoughts, but before he had a chance to say anything, the front door opened. He smiled and nodded at both Elliott and Doc.

"We didn't miss dinner, did we?" Elliott asked in a booming voice. He walked over to the stove and took a look in the pot.

"I'm gonna go look in on Cecily. I'll be back in a few minutes for dinner." Doc nodded at them all and went into Cecily's room.

"I hope she's well enough to sleep on the floor. I want my room back."

"For heavens sakes, Lucy, she's bleeding and in pain. You only think about yourself. You need to learn to have compassion for others." Shane frowned at her and shook his head.

"Well it sure smells good. I didn't know you were such a good cook, Lucy," Elliott said as a smile spread across his face. He glanced at Shane and winked at him letting him know he was trying to defuse the situation. Shane gave him an almost imperceptible nod back.

"I'll set the table," Poor Boy announced.

He was probably excited to get dinner over so he could spend time with Cecily and Shane didn't blame him one bit. In fact, he wished he had an excuse to spend more time with her too.

"Do you need any help, Lucy?" Shane asked. He watched

as Elliott sat in the chair and stretched his long legs out in front of him.

"Well, now is a fine time to ask. I've slaved over this stove for hours." Lucy turned, put her hands on her hips and gave him a sour look.

"Heck, Cecily had a lot of it done. I'm asking if you need help now. You know, you're not helping the situation any by being so crabby."

Lucy's mouth formed an O. "Let me tell you something, Shane, I traveled forever to get here to see you again. I've gone out of my way to be kind to the two misfits you have living here, and what do I get? I get chastised like a child. Shane, if you had bothered to look, I am very much a woman now. I came out here so we could get married and start a family. It's what I've wanted ever since I can remember. We used to be so close, and now it is almost as though you can't stand me."

Before he could answer, Doc came out of Cecily's room, took some soap out of his bag, and went outside to the water pump to wash his hands. Shane ran his fingers through his hair and realized that they had a rapt audience. Elliott and Poor Boy stared at them.

"Married? I think I do remember you from the O'Conner plantation." Elliott stood and walked over to Lucy. Lucy's eyes widened in fear as she caught Shane's gaze.

"Lucy is my cousin. Lucy attended many parties at my home. Perhaps you danced with her." Shane wasn't sure he was convincing enough.

"I did dance with you didn't I, Lucy?" Elliott looked her up and down before he sat back down.

Now Shane had to keep Elliott off of Lucy's trail. Dang it, what were the odds they'd both be here at the same time?

The doc came back in all smiles. "It sure does smell good in here, and I'm mighty hungry."

Poor Boy tilted his head as he stared at the doctor. "Does Cecily get to eat too?"

Doc chuckled softly. "Yes, she gets to eat too. Lucy, would you mind putting a portion aside for Cecily? It would probably be better to let it cool down a bit. You could help her after dinner." Doc sat down and looked around the room. "I remember when they built this place. It really is a shame the Ashers never got to live in it. Yes, we lost a lot of good people to diphtheria."

Lucy served the food and dropped into her seat as though exhausted. "Well, by golly, it's been a long day."

Doc put a big spoonful of food into his mouth, swallowed, and began to talk. "This is good. Thank you kindly."

Shane wasn't happy with the look of disgust Lucy gave to Doc. "You're right, this sure is good." He stood and nodded to them all. "If you'll excuse me I'd like to make sure Cecily gets something to eat."

Lucy pursed her lips as her eyes narrowed. "The polite thing to do would be to wait until after everyone is finished."

Shane's eyes widened. "This is my house, and I do not need a lesson or instruction in manners. I'm assuming Cecily just had some laudanum." He looked at the doctor and waited for him to nod his head. "She needs food in her stomach before she falls asleep. I don't feel the need to explain my actions to anyone." He picked up the plate and grabbed a spoon before he went into Cecily's room. His voice had gotten a bit loud, but doggone it, this was his house and Lucy had best learn not to push him.

His tension fled as soon as he saw Cecily. She lay on the bed and her back was still exposed. She turned her head and smiled when she saw him. She started to move and grimaced.

"Hey sweetheart, don't go hurting yourself. You lay as still as you can. I brought you something to eat. I just need to figure out how to get it into your mouth without making a huge mess." He walked over to the bed and placed the food on the side table and then leaned down, giving her a kiss on the cheek. Her face turned a beautiful shade of red, and his heart sped up. Just being around her made him happy. It was the type of happiness he didn't understand, finding joy in the little things, and he'd never felt that before.

Shane knelt down on the floor and lifted the plate of food off the table. He looked from the dish to her mouth then back to the dish again. "I think it best I go get a towel in case I spill." He put the plate back on the table then stood and left the room.

"Well that sure was fast," Elliott commented as he cocked his left brow.

"Just grabbing a towel so we don't have to wash the sheets." Before anyone replied, Shane picked up a towel and headed back to Cecily.

Her eyes had begun to close, and he could see she was fighting to stay awake.

He placed the towel under her head and shoulder and sat back down on the floor. "Darlin', I need you to eat. Laudanum on an empty stomach is worse than any rotgut you can find. Plus you need to eat to keep up your strength."

She shook her head a bit and he reached out and smoothed her hair away from her face. "You know, this will go much easier with your cooperation." He smiled when she nodded. He scooped a bit of the stew onto the spoon and tried to angle it into her mouth. The first spoonful was a success but not the second. Rich brown liquid dribbled from the corner of her mouth. "I sure am glad I put the towel down."

"You make me forget my pain, and I thank you. No one has ever done that for me before; no one has ever tried. So now you know my back is all scarred, and I bet it's hideous to look at. John Hardy stole so much from me by pretending

I was going to be his mail order bride.I was used to pay a debt. It's almost as though they forgot that I'm really a person. A very, very naïve person. As soon as I'm well I'm going to leave. Now don't say a word, it's just something I have to do. It's bad enough people staring at me thinking they know what happened, but I don't think I could take people actually knowing the truth of my torture. A new town, new surroundings, and new people will be good for me." Tears began to fall down her lovely face.

A lump formed in Shane's throat. "Sometimes there just ain't nothing you can do. Unfortunately, you have no control over your situation, and I'm sorry for that. I want you to think about staying and helping me build this farm, because without you my heart wouldn't be in it." He took a deep breath and let it out slowly. Part of him understood her decision, and part of him wished she'd declare she wanted to stay with him.

"No more food please." Her voice was husky with sleep. He watched as she struggled to keep her eyes open. After setting the plate of food back on the table he sat on the bed next to her and stroked her hair. She sure had beautiful silky hair. The thought of losing her made his stomach quiver, and he was at a loss of what to do next. She wouldn't be going anywhere for at least a week maybe more. After her back healed he just didn't know and that saddened him. It was true sometimes there was just nothing a person could do.

CHAPTER SEVEN

One week later

Cecily's eyes suddenly opened wide, and her body tensed. Where was she and how had she gotten there? She needed to escape and fast. Frantically, she looked around the best she could in the dark and found her dress. After she slipped it on, she located a shawl, disappointed to discover the room was windowless. She had to get out of there, she just had to. She snuck out the bedroom, tiptoed through the kitchen down the hall to the front of the house. Slowly and as quietly as she could she opened the door, stepped through, and closed it behind her.

Then she ran as fast as she could. She ran across the canyon floor and headed for the shortcut. The woods there made a good hiding place. She couldn't allow them to get her, not again. Her feet stung as she flew over the rocky earth. She'd forgotten her shoes. It didn't matter now, though. She couldn't go back, she refused to go back to be tortured. Her back was on fire, and her soul was battered beyond repair. She kept going, increasing her pace.

She found the shortcut and went through the canyon wall

until she came out on the other side. The first thing she did was to locate the densest part of the forest. That was where she ran to. Her heart beat so fast, and she was gulping air, her lungs burning, but she refused to stop. Long Nose would surely kill her this time. Tears ran down her face. This would be her last night on earth. How would he do it? Would he simply drive the knife into her heart? She found a big tree and squatted beside it, hiding.

No, a knife would be too quick, and Long Nose liked to drag things out, especially pain. He seemed to enjoy the sound of her screams. Every time she ran away, they always caught her, somehow. The punishments were so horrendous. She put both hands over her mouth to silence her sobs. The last time they'd caught her, he'd burned her back with flaming pieces of wood. Never had anything been so agonizing.

Finally, she quieted herself. She needed to think. Boy, was she tired. She found some downed branches and placed them over her. There, she was hidden. She listened to the night sounds of animals scurrying about. At one point a raccoon stood in front of her and it seemed to be scolding her.

The pain in her back was unbearable. The smile Long Nose had given her sent chills of terror through her body. She wrapped her arms around herself as some form of protection, not that it ever worked. What had she done to deserve such torment and pain? She dug her nails into her palms until it hurt, wishing it was Long Nose she was hurting instead. Her body shook as her mind whirled. She couldn't get the atrocities laid upon her out of her memory. What type of husband used a woman and then threw her on the ground offering her to others?

Her back burned and burned. There was no way she was going to be able to stay in her hiding spot; it hurt her back too much. Closing her eyes for a moment, she dozed.

It was just before dawn when she awoke, and her confusion was great. Where was she? She must've had one of her awful dreams. She'd never be like a normal woman, and it was time to give up trying. She could only be herself, a woman with a battered soul and body. Carefully, she sat up, not without a groan or two, and pushed the branches away from her. She stood and turned in a big circle, trying to find some type of landmark she recognized. Her shoulders slumped. There was no such landmark.

The woods were too dense for her to find the canyon, and it was hard to tell which way the sun was coming. Her best bet would be to get out of the forest, but how? Taking a deep breath she decided upon a direction and began to walk. Rocks, broken branches, and pine needles all drove into her feet with every step she took. She tried to move as silently as she could, afraid there were more Indians out there. How she had run so far last night, she'd never know.

Rustling in the underbrush made her pause. She knew it was either a bear or a man. Her heart stopped as she strained to listen, but she'd been so turned around she wasn't sure where the sound was coming from. She pressed her back against the big tree and began to tremble. She glanced around her looking for a tree she could climb in case it was a bear.

She found the perfect tree and decided man or bear she was going to climb it and get out of sight. It didn't take long to shimmy up the tree and find a branch to perch on. The leaves covered her presence, and now all she could do was wait.

It wasn't much longer before Shane wandered into view, head down, studying the ground as he walked. Cecily sighed in relief. She'd been certain her fate was to be a meal for a bear. To her surprise, Lucy was right behind him tramping through the woods. If not for her, Cecily probably would never have heard Shane until he was right behind her. She was about to let herself down when Lucy began to nag at him.

"You're going too fast. I'm getting tired," Lucy whined.

"I told you not to come. Cecily is none of your business," Shane said impatiently.

"Well, I couldn't very well stay at the house and have Elliott stare at me, now could I?"

"You must have known the risk of trying to be someone you're not. These are still trying times, and even though you're no longer a slave, people still have their prejudices. I told you before I'll keep your secret, but I'm not going to boot Elliott out of the house."

"I just wanted a better life. I wanted you. I thought you and I had something special, so wonderful that you'd be happy to see me. It never occurred to me you didn't feel that way."

"I lied to you. My father had a very good reason for us to stay apart. He thought we were becoming too close, and he had made arrangements to sell you. I left instead."

"A good reason? I don't understand what you're saying."

"You're my sister."

Lucy gasped. "What are you talking about? Are you telling me your father and my mother...? No... I—I don't feel so good. Let's keep walking get this over with." Lucy's heartbreak was evident in her voice.

Cecily watched as they walked away, surprised by the new development. Lucy looked white and from the way she'd seen people treat the ex-slaves, she didn't blame her one bit. Poor Lucy. She'd loved someone her whole life only to find out it was a forbidden love. Life wasn't fair. Cecily climbed down the tree and began to walk in the direction Shane and Lucy had taken.

SHANE RUBBED the back of his neck as he glanced at Lucy. The devastation on her face was a kick to his gut. They'd been childhood friends, but he'd known all along they'd never have a future. "I know it's a shock, Lucy. I was overwhelmed and surprised when I found out. I suppose that's why he always kept you in the house, so he could watch you grow."

Lucy shrugged her shoulders but refused to look at him. "Well there's nothing I can do. I can't believe I spent so much time in love with a man who is really my brother. I thought you left because your daddy wouldn't let you have me. I'm not sure what to do now."

Her voice was so flat Shane grew concerned. Then he heard a noise. He suddenly grabbed Lucy one arm around her waist and his other hand over her mouth and pulled her off the trail. "Someone's following us, you need to be silent," he whispered. He waited until she nodded in understanding before he took his hand away from her mouth.

Whoever it was, wasn't trying to be quiet, and the more he listened, the more he became convinced it was Cecily trailing behind them. He wanted to run in her direction and scoop her up, hugging her to his body. He wanted to kiss her until she promised never to leave again, but he couldn't do that with Lucy watching.

"I'm pretty sure it's Cecily," he whispered. "You stay here, I'll be right back."

Lucy nodded, but her widened eyes shared her fear. He felt bad for having to leave her. "It'll only be a minute."

Shane walked back the way they had come and sure enough, Cecily was shuffling toward him. Relief swept his body as he watched her. She came to him and stood right in front of him toe to toe standing silently as she caught his gaze and held it.

After a while, she spoke. "Thank you. Thank you for coming out here to find me." He studied her scratched face and hands. Her hair was full of twigs and leaves while her dress had tiny rips here and there. The circles under her eyes were very dark and she looked like she'd been through hell.

"Sweetheart, are you alright? It looks like you wrestled with a grizzly." He took her hands in his and leaned down, giving her a kiss on the cheek.

"I had another dream, a nightmare. It all seemed so real. I was so frightened that I kept running and ended up lost."

"I figured as much. Lucy's not far, we need to go get her." He released one of Cecily's hands but held onto the other as he took a step forward. He heard her gasp as she walked and looked down at her bare feet. "You didn't think to bring your shoes?"

"I guess I was in a hurry." She looked at the ground refusing to catch his gaze. Shane quickly gathered her up in his arms and carried her down the trail to where Lucy waited. Lucy looked none too happy when they finally met up with her. She had her arms crossed while she tapped her foot with the most sour look on her face.

"Oh good, you found her. Now we can go home. I think we'll need to lock you in the room. We can't have you traipsing all over God knows where, leaving Shane to go find you. He needs his rest too, you know, and I think it's highly inconsiderate for you to play this juvenile hide-and-seek game with him. Come on, let's get going." Lucy marched down the trail, her steps so haughty, Shane wanted to laugh.

"Lucy, you're going the wrong way."

She turned and gave them an exaggerated sigh while she shook her head. "Of course I am," she said with sarcasm dripping from each word. She put her hands on her hips and marched on by them while giving them the look of the devil.

Shane thought it best not to say a word. Lucy was too riled up as it was, and he didn't want her using her razor-sharp tongue on Cecily. He walked, cradling Cecily against his body, and he was filled with a sense of rightness, a sense of belonging, and a sense of peace he hadn't felt in a very long time. He was going to end up with a broken heart; he knew it, and there was nothing he could do about it. Cecily wouldn't want another man to touch her. She'd suffered too much already, and he didn't blame her for being afraid. He turned his head and looked at her face and his heart beat wildly when she met his gaze and smiled.

They were making pretty good time and were just about to the canyon and the hidden trail, when Lucy abruptly stopped. She stood blocking the entrance, giving them both a scathing look. "You could probably put her down now. I don't know why you're carrying her, and it certainly does not look right. I really think it's for the best if Cecily moved to a different town and started over."

Shane gritted his teeth and counted to ten before he answered her. "I happen to think it's best if Cecily stays. I can give her all the protection she needs."

Lucy shook her head. "You stupid fool. Don't you realize the whole town is talking about you behind your back? Everyone has an opinion as to why she is staying in your house and some of the opinions are downright nasty. Don't you see she's dragging you down, and you don't need that? You need someone in your life who is above approach, someone who is clean and pure. Cecily is neither of those things. In fact, she is quite the opposite. She has lain with dirty Indians and allowed them unspeakable liberties. Why, in the eyes of the good people of Asherville, she is no better than a dog."

Shane felt his shirt grow wet as Cecily silently cried. "Lucy, why don't you go on ahead to the house and pack your things. Edith Mathers has a room above the mercantile she might be able to rent to you while you wait for the stage to come through. You never once gave Cecily a chance and if you had, you'd know that she is a fine, loving, giving woman. And I don't believe the whole town is saying those things, a few maybe but not most. Goodbye, Lucy."

Lucy's jaw dropped and her eyes widened. She looked as though she'd never seen him before. She shook her head before she spoke. "You'll be sorry, Shane, I know you will be. You may talk a good game but you know what I said is true. You may think you have feelings for her, but she has you bamboozled. I think that's why she keeps running into the woods. She's looking for the band of Indians her husband lived with. If she was so perfect, she'd be content to stay in your house. Mark my words, she will leave at the first sign of those heathens."

He didn't flinch. In fact, he didn't care what she had to say. All he wanted was Lucy out of his sight and out of his life. He never had figured out what her game was or how she had come by such fancy clothes, but it really didn't matter.

Lucy narrowed her eyes as she stared at Cecily. Suddenly, she turned and with her back straight she walked through the canyon wall.

Shane carried Cecily to a nearby creek and set her down on the bank. She put her feet into the water and smiled. "Thank you."

He dropped down next to her and all was silent except for the bubbling of the creek. There was so much he wished he could say but he'd end up playing the fool. "How is your back? I kept thinking about how much pain you were in and the smell of blood…"

Cecily covered her mouth with her hand as her eyes grew

wide. "It never occurred to me. I was out of my mind. I was reliving Long Nose coming after me. I ran away a few times, until he burned my back. After that if he thought I looked at him wrong he threw me on the ground and burned me again." She dropped her hand as she closed her eyes. "I'm surprised a wolf or a bear didn't finish me off last night."

"I was scared to death to find you gone. I had hoped you'd feel safe at the house." He gave her a semblance of a smile. Disappointment engulfed him.

Reaching out she grasped his hand with hers. "I do. I feel safe with you. I think I had more of that nasty medicine than usual. I remember you giving me some after I ate but then later…" Cecily shrugged. "I just don't know. Everything turned into a strange dream and it was so real to me."

He stood and pulled her up. "Let's get you home where you belong."

CHAPTER EIGHT

$\mathcal{W}$ithin a week, both Lucy and Elliott were gone. Cecily had no idea where they went or if they went together. Lucy never inquired about the room above the mercantile. No one had seen them leave, and it was puzzling. Cecily's back was still painful, and Doc stopped by just in time for dinner to tend to her. Shane treated her with kid gloves, and she wasn't quite sure whether she liked it or not. On one hand, it was nice to have his attention but on the other hand, she wasn't a helpless ninny. The ground had been tilled, and tomorrow she would begin to plant. It was something she'd been looking forward to.

Poor Boy came rushing into the kitchen, gasping for breath. "They've come to get you Cecily, we better hide!"

She dropped the towel she'd been holding. Her heart began to pound. "What do you mean who're 'they'?"

"There's a band of Indians headed this way, and I heard talk that they were Long Nose's Indians. I've got to hide you. Shane said so."

Automatically, she grabbed the shotgun, all the shells she

could carry, locked the door, shuttered the windows and shooed Poor Boy into the root cellar. She followed him down and locked the door. Thank goodness she had finished her rag rug. She just hoped that it would hide the opening to the root cellar. They could hear horse hooves pounding upon the earth. Her hands began to shake, but she managed to get the shotgun loaded.

Poor Boy curled up in the corner, and he covered his head with his hands. Somehow, she'd have to make sure they were safe. She looked around, wishing she'd found the time to explore and locate the other entrance she was convinced existed somewhere. She lit a lamp and began to inspect each wall. Most were lined with shelves of supplies. She didn't see anything on her first pass through, so she stood in the middle of the room perfectly still waiting to feel the fresh air. It was coming from behind the shelves with the many lanterns on it.

The shattering of glass above drove a spike of fear into her heart. She knew that laughter it belonged to Choked Bear, Long Nose's best friend. She froze for a second and then forced herself to snap out of it. She grabbed Poor Boy by the hand and together they pushed on the shelf. To her relief, it swung open into a very narrow passageway. It was filled with cobwebs, but she didn't care. Better a spider than Choked Bear. Heightened excitement filled their voices, and the door to the root cellar rattled. She grabbed an extra lantern, snatched up her shotgun, and pushed Poor Boy into the passage. It was surprisingly easy to close the door to the passageway.

"Where are we going, Cecily?" Poor Boy asked as his voice shook.

"I don't know where this leads, but we need to be very quiet. They mustn't find us here." She nudged Poor Boy forward. They walked slowly and silently as the cobwebs swept over their faces down the long passageway. Cecily kept looking over her shoulder half expecting to see Choked Bear behind her.

Finally they came to the end of the tunnel. Poor Boy pushed against the wall and when the door opened, he turned and grabbed her around the waist in fear.

Cecily urged him forward and they stepped into a room filled with barrels of beer and casks of whiskey. Cecily closed the door behind her and sagged against one of the barrels. It looks as though Mr. Asher wanted to be able to go to the saloon without anyone else knowing. Probably his wife.

"Now what?" Poor Boy asked with worry written all over his face. Cecily put down the lanterns and her shotgun and then hugged Poor Boy to her.

"I suppose we alert someone upstairs and have them get word to Shane that we're safe." Poor Boy stepped out of her embrace and nodded. They started up the stairs when they heard mumbling and grumbling about the Indians. One man was all for using them for target practice while another wanted to hand Cecily over so they'd go away.

Cecily stood on the step afraid to go farther. "Poor Boy, I need you to find Miss Noreen and let her know we're safe and that we have to get the message to Shane."

Poor Boy shook his head crossed his arms and went back down the stairs. She followed him back down. "You don't like my plan?"

The expression on Poor Boy's face was one of the hard headed mule. "Is something wrong? Why won't you go up there?"

He looked everywhere in the cellar except at her and took a deep breath. "I don't like this place. Before I found Eats, John Hardy had me working here. All he did was backhand me and punch me, and the customers were just as bad."

"Poor Boy, I'm so sorry, but John Hardy is dead. I say

good riddance. He was an awful man who hurt a lot of people. But he's not here. Noreen owns the place now, and she's a nice woman. I'd go myself but you heard how some of them would like to exchange me for the Indians leaving, and I can't let that happen. Most of all I don't want Shane going after the Indians thinking they have us. They'll kill him."

Poor Boy bit his top lip and for a moment she thought he'd refuse. Then he took a deep breath and nodded. "You can count on me, Cecily." He slowly climbed the stairs, and Cecily said a prayer when he was out of sight.

It seemed to take forever, and Cecily couldn't help but think that Poor Boy had gotten in some kind of trouble. The sight of Noreen coming down the steps relieved her worry and she quickly took the saloon owner's offered hand. They slowly went up the steps and then Noreen smuggled her down the hall to a stairway leading to the second floor.

"Poor Boy is waiting for you in room three. Don't you worry, I have someone going after Shane, and the rest of the town is armed and ready. There's been a lot of talk about just giving you to the Indians. No matter what, don't leave the room." Noreen let go of her hand and shooed her up the stairs.

Cecily quickly opened the door to room three and closed it behind her. She leaned her back against it and braced herself as Poor Boy came flying at her, hugging her tightly. "We have to be quiet. Noreen sent somebody after Shane. All we can do now is wait and hope."

FLAMES REACHED INTO THE SKY, and the scent of charred wood filled the air, as Shane watched in shock while his house burned. There'd been no sign of Cecily or Poor Boy, and all he could think was they were either dead or captives. Not many of the Indians had gotten away, and he was more inclined to think they were dead. His heart squeezed so painfully, his emotions became raw. He'd never even told Cecily how he felt about her. Dammit, he had let her go on thinking that no man would ever want her and he should've set her straight from the very first. He wanted her. He figured Poor Boy would eventually go back to Eats, but if he hadn't he would have always had a home with Shane.

Wood still burned as the structure tumbled leaving fiery embers in its place. He couldn't look away, he just couldn't. He'd always remember this was the place where his love died. Misery settled around him and he was oblivious to the others watching with him. Cinders, Keegan, and Cookie had all come out to help. They were good men they were good friends. The fact that they let him be and didn't say a word meant a lot to him. Did they kill Cecily and Poor Boy before the house was set on fire or did they just let them burn alive? He got off his horse went to the closest bush and was sick.

He felt a hand on his shoulder and when he turned he tried to give Keegan a semblance of a smile but he knew he failed. "They're dead, Keegan, they're dead. Funny isn't it? I should've been the one person who could have protected them, and I didn't."

Keegan opened his mouth but closed it again as another man from town rode hell-bent straight toward them.

"Sheriff! Noreen sent me. Miss Cecily and Poor Boy are both fine," the young man said in a breathless rush of words.

"Were they at the saloon?" Shane didn't wait for an answer he jumped on his horse and in a flash headed toward town. He barely waited for Jester to slow in front of the saloon before he jumped down. He ran through the swinging doors and looked wildly around the room.

"Shane, this way," Noreen yelled out as she gestured toward the stairs. "Room three."

He didn't have time to thank Noreen as he ran up the rest of the stairs and burst into the room. His heart beat wildly, and he was out of breath as he stood in the doorway. A more wonderful sight he'd never seen. Cecily and Poor Boy sat on the bed clutching each other, eyes wide with stark terror. He took one step in and opened his arms. It hardly took any time at all before Cecily clung to him. He held her with one arm and opened the other arm to Poor Boy who joined their embrace.

"Dear Lord, I thought I'd lost you both. It's a miracle you survived, and I'm grateful." He felt tears forming behind his eyes and try as he might to keep them at bay, they trailed down his face as he held Cecily and Poor Boy close. Poor Boy was the first to step out of the embrace, and then Cecily took a step back too.

"I wasn't sure we'd make it. I had a feeling there was another entrance to the huge root cellar under the house, and I'm so glad I was right. Behind one of the shelves was a passageway. We followed it for a long time and we ended up here at the saloon. I wonder why they built it? Actually I have my suspicions. It certainly did save our lives." She gave Shane the sweetest smile ever.

Shane tried to dry his eyes to no avail. His emotions got the best of him and he couldn't help himself. "There's so much I want to tell you, so much I thought I missed telling you because you were dead."

Cecily stepped closer to him and stroked his whiskered cheek with her fingers. "There's no need for you to say anything. I had the same fear in my heart when I thought of you out there fighting Indians. That's how it is with friends, they care about each other."

The breath whooshed from Shane's lungs; he was pole axed. They were talking about two different things. He talked of love, and she talked of friendship. He had hoped, he'd thought, and he'd gotten it all wrong.

"Can I go out and see all the action?" Poor Boy asked gesturing toward the door.

"Go right ahead. It should be safe by now."

"Thanks Shane, see you later, Cecily." Poor Boy ran from the room.

Shane sat down on the bed and drew Cecily down onto his lap. He tucked her head under his chin and held her close, savoring the feel of her next to him. Why couldn't she feel the same way? He'd have to take what she offered and be grateful, but it was going to be damn hard. He stroked her arm for a while then pulled back from her just enough for him to put finger under her chin and lift her face to his. He stared into her beautiful brown eyes, and his heart jolted. It wasn't friendship he saw shining in her eyes, it was love. Perhaps she didn't really know how she felt.

He kept her head tilted as he lowered his until their lips touched. He waited for her to pull away or to gasp and protest, but she did neither, so he continued kissing her. Her plump, soft lips were a treat to him, and he knew he'd never get tired of kissing her. Somewhere along the line she snaked her arms around his neck, and when he moved to take a break from their kiss, she pulled him back down to her mouth for more delightful kisses. She was the sweetest sweet, and he sure wished she was his.

She finally broke off the kiss and let go of his neck. As she drew back, she stared at him with wonder in her eyes. "That was the nicest kiss I've ever had. Thank you." Her expression changed from one of wonder to one of wistfulness. Then he realized she didn't understand his intent. Nothing was ever easy when a female is involved. He'd have to come up with another way of showing her his love for her.

CECILY STOOD and walked to the window, drawing the curtain open with hands that shook. There was so much whirling around in her head it was hard to think. It was late afternoon and she needed to find a place to spend the night. The saloon was not the answer, but then again her reputation was so bad already... She glanced over her shoulder and admired Shane's profile. Even covered in soot and ash, he was a handsome devil. His kiss had awakened something inside of her, and she wasn't sure what it was. Sadly, she'd never find out. Sighing, she looked out the window again. Where would she go from here? Shane could stay at the jailhouse. Someone was bound to take Poor Boy in. That left her.

Swallowing hard, she turned around and tried to smile at Shane, but her lips trembled.

Shane instantly rose from the bed and came to her side. He reached up and tucked a wayward lock of hair behind her ear. "You've had to be brave through all this, and I bet you're tired."

"I just do what needs to be done, that's all. There's no special bravery involved." She studied his face, and she could easily see the worry he bore. It was like looking into his soul. He had enough problems of his own he didn't need the extra burden of her. "I guess this will be goodbye. I hate to ask, but do you think you can pay me for the few days I worked?"

Shane frowned. "Of course I can pay you. Just what is it you're planning to do? You're not leaving town, are you?" Shane took her hand and held it tight, caressing the back of it with his thumb. I know the house burned down and things might look a little grim right now, but I plan to rebuild, and my plans include you."

She lowered her head and stared at their linked hands. It would be so easy to believe that everything was going to be okay, but the plain truth was, she was homeless and not many doors would be open to her for the night. "Shane, rebuilding takes time, lots of time. I don't think you thought this all through. I'll need some place to stay, and although I like Shannon and Addy, they have families of their own. There's no way Edith would allow me to stay above the mercantile."

"Then, my sweet, we will just do it pioneer style."

Her gaze met his, and she could see the merriment in his eyes. "Just what are you planning?" She couldn't help the smile that spread across her face. "What exactly do you mean by pioneer style?"

"We have animals to tend, the garden to nurture and a crop of something to put in. We'll need to be on the property to be able to do it all. I have an idea and that's all I'm going to say. Tell you what. I'll have Noreen send up some tea for you while I arrange everything."

"You're not going to leave me here all night, are you?"

"Of course not. I promise to be back well before dark." Shane let go of her hand and then leaned down and gave her a heart-stopping kiss. Her lips still tingled long after he left the room. She just hoped he wasn't making any false promises.

SHANE HURRIED through the back door of the saloon and up the stairs to room number three. He opened the door and gave Cecily a great big smile. His smile faded as he saw the tears in her eyes. He took a few steps until he stood toe to toe with her and then he wiped away a trailing tear with his thumb. Framing her face with his hands he kissed her soft lips. He stared into her eyes for a moment before he pulled her close and wrapped her in his arms.

"Everything's going to be fine, you'll see." He kissed the top of her head and then let her go. "Come with me." He took her hand and led her out of the saloon. He tried to pretend the whole town wasn't watching them walking along the wooden walkway hand in hand. But he could tell by the way Cecily stiffened that she noticed it too.

The air was full of the acrid smell of burned wood, and smoke could still be seen coming from where their house used to be. Cecily looked up at him her eyes full of questions but he just shrugged. Finally, as they got closer to the property, she seemed to relax.

"I guess when you said pioneer you really meant pioneer," Cecily commented with a hint of laughter in her voice.

They stood together and stared at the covered wagon and tent set up not too far from the original dwelling. A fire pit had been dug, and everything she would need to cook over a fire was in a crate next to a big pile of firewood.

"So, what do you think? You sleep in the wagon, and I'll sleep in the tent. Before you think I'm crazy, it's safe. Cinders tracked the last Comanche from the raid and he'd died of his wounds. And I've already received a great number of offers to help get the house rebuilt. What do you think?" Cecily waited so long to answer his heart skipped a beat and his stomach tightened. It was the best he could do, and he had hoped it would be good enough for her. He dropped her hand and put his hands in his pockets. "Well, I guess that's it, I'll take you out to Cinders' place."

Cecily put her hands on her hips and stared at him. "You most certainly will not be taking me to Cinders' place. I can be a pioneer. As a matter of fact, I bet I can be the best darn pioneer you ever knew. You do realize I'm only staying because of the cow, and of course the garden."

"Lucky for me I bought that cow." Shane put his hands on her waist, lifted her up, and twirled her around. His heart filled with joy, and he felt as though they were on the verge of something very special.

CHAPTER NINE

Shane whistled as he walked down the boardwalk toward his office. Once he entered, he poured himself a cup coffee, sat in his chair, and put his feet up on the desk. After a couple of sips, he picked up a stack of wanted posters he'd meant to get to weeks ago. He laughed at a couple of the posters. The men on them looked so mean and nasty, and he would bet that wasn't how they looked at all. One caught his eye, and he recognized the man as one of the gamblers. He quickly rifled through a few more posters before he found the other gambler, the one who'd shot him. He stared at the posters for a while. They weren't just gamblers, they were bank robbers. According to one poster, there were four members in the gang, with one of them being a woman.

He anxiously looked through the rest of the pile for the posters of the other two bank robbers, but there weren't any. Shaking his head at the inconvenience, he left the jailhouse and walked down to the telegraph office, where he sent a telegram inquiring about the description of the other two. The answer came fast and with a sinking heart, he realized the descriptions fit Elliott and Lucy to perfection. They had to be the other half of the gang. He blew out a frustrated breath. How stupid could he have been? He'd welcomed both of them with open arms. They had acted as though they didn't know one another. The town didn't have much of a bank, so what had they been doing in Asherville?

He next went to the saloon and smiled politely at the girls who worked there while he waited for Noreen to come down. At last, she made a grand entrance and practically squealed in delight that he wanted to see her. Her frown was equally exaggerated when he told her he needed to ask her some questions.

"We might as well use my office," Noreen said as she batted her eyelashes at him.

Shane followed her down the hall and into an ornate office. All the pieces of furniture were oversized and finely crafted. Probably from when John Hardy had owned the saloon. He sat in the offered chair and watched as she went behind her desk and sat down.

"So tell me why the well-respected sheriff needs to talk to me?"

"Those gamblers, you remember them, don't you?" He waited for her to nod. "They were actually bank robbers, and since we really don't have a bank for them to rob, I wonder why they were here in town. After all, Asherville isn't a very prosperous town. You don't happen to know anything about them, do you?"

She stared at her hands, fiddling with her fingernails. Yes, she knew something.

He cocked one eyebrow. "Hmmm?"

After a moment, Noreen's shoulders sagged. "They were here to meet up with the rest of their gang. They assured me that nobody in Asherville would be hurt, and they paid me to keep my mouth shut."

"And the rest of the gang were…?"

Noreen waved her hand in the air. "How would I know? Something about they'd pulled a job and all planned to meet here. The only other strangers around were your two friends. *They* seemed to be searching for something. The man, Elliot, asked a lot of questions. Listen, sheriff that's all I know. Are we done here?"

Shane stood and nodded. Without another word, he walked out of the saloon. He'd never had all that much respect for Noreen, but now he had none. She had knowingly put the town at risk. She could've tipped him off before he got shot, but her greed had gotten in the way. He groaned aloud. What a headache. He could kick himself for giving Lucy and Elliott a place to stay. How stupid did one man have to be? Lucy'd never loved him. She was too selfish to love anyone. They played him all right, pretending not to know each other. What a fool he'd been, a stupid fool.

He went back to the telegraph office and sent information about Lucy and Elliott off to the Texas Rangers. Those two would have a hard time finding a place to stay from now on. With his mission complete, he left the telegraph office. All he wanted to do was see was Cecily's smile, hear her voice.

And enough was enough. He had something he wanted to ask her.

He strode to their pioneer set up and stopped before Cecily saw him. He wanted to gaze at her and enjoy her smile. When she spotted him, her smile grew wider, and she hurried toward him. When she was within reach, he grabbed her up into his arms and kissed her. He loved the blush that spread across her face. As he set her down, he grabbed her hand and led her toward the camp.

"Sit," he said, pointing to one of the chairs. Holding her gaze, he knelt on one knee in front of her.

"What's all this?" Cecily asked, an expression of bewilderment on her face.

"I've a question I want to ask you. I've been staring at you the last few days trying to figure out if you are happy with me or not. I've come to the conclusion that you are, and if I'm right and you are, will you marry me?" His heart beat so fast and loud in his ears.

"The answer is no. I'm so sorry." Cecily rose to her feet and ran in the direction of the creek. His heart dropped, and he thought he might be sick. He was nothing but a damn fool.

But fool or not, he needed to talk to her and reassure her that she still had a place to live.

He finally found her under a cottonwood tree with her bare feet dangling in the water. Any other time he would've thought her enchanting, but now he just wanted to salvage their friendship. He sat down on the grass next to her, took off his shoes, and put his feet into the water as well.

Finally after an interminable silence Shane turned to her. "I'm sorry. I shouldn't have proposed to you. You probably never want to be with a man again, and I should've remembered that. I should've remembered how Long Nose tortured you, and I should've remembered your nightmares. I have feelings for you, and I'm not sure what to do with them but I don't want you to leave. I want us to have the farm and everything you've dreamed of."

Cecily reached over and put her hand on top of his. "I don't know if I can be a proper wife. I just really don't know. Besides I have hideous burn marks. You deserve a woman who is well respected in the community and untouched. I have feelings for you too, more than I ever thought I could have for any man but it's simply not fair to you." She turned her head toward him and tears poured down her face. She hiccupped then buried her face in her hands.

"I don't want somebody else. I want you, and if you never feel that you can be intimate with me I'll live with it, I swear I will. I want to know that every day I'm coming home to you."

She sat back up and stared out at the creek. "That's what you do every day you come home to me. You'll lose your job if you marry me. People don't approve of me."

"I don't care about other people, and I don't care if they fire me. I want to be able to lay next to you and hold you in my arms. You, not some woman others approve of. Want to reconsider?" He held his breath waiting for her to answer and finally she put her head on his shoulder.

"You're offering me everything I've ever wanted. You're right, we should do what's best for us not what's best for the Ediths of the world. I love you with everything inside me. Sometimes I feel like I'm going to explode holding in my love for you. I suppose if we take it slow, we'll eventually have a family of our own."

Hope quickened in his chest. "You're saying yes aren't you?"

She giggled. "Oh yes, I'm saying yes."

$\mathcal{I}$t had taken longer than he'd wanted to build a home. But finally it was finished. It wasn't as big as the one that burned, but it didn't matter. Cecily was all that mattered. Her happiness was his happiness. The last few weeks had been a blur.

With the knowledge he'd provided the Texas Rangers, the law had quickly caught up to Elliot and Lucy. He supposed he should have felt bad, but he didn't. He did, however, continue to kick himself for welcoming them into his house. Cecily told him it just showed how kind his heart was. He argued that he was just plain stupid.

He peered around. From the front of the house, he could see the town, the canyon, and the wonderful piece of land he and Cecily had nourished and brought to life. He'd imagined a small garden but the one she planted could feed half the town. It made her happy, so he helped take care of it.

They built a bigger chicken coop with Poor Boy's help. He looked mighty fine in his best clothes. Shane offered him a home, but Eats had begun construction on a new restaurant, and Poor Boy wanted to stay with him. He looked rested, and Cecily commented how his nightmares must have stopped.

It was a fine day for a wedding. Cecily had tried to call it off more than once. Her nerves about the wedding night had gotten the better of her, and he could tell she wanted to run. He just held her in his arms and told her not to worry. Of course he would have loved a family but not everyone got to be parents.

He smiled when Cinders and Keegan came to shake his hand. "The big day. How you holding up?" Cinders asked.

"Better than I thought. I'm more worried she'll change her mind."

Keegan nodded his sympathy. "Women keep you guessing to the very end. Looks like the ceremony is going to begin, I'd better find Addy."

It was quiet, very quiet and he sighed in relief when he caught sight of his beautiful bride. Shannon had outdone herself by making the dress. It was perfect. It made Cecily look like a dream. He'd never been prouder watching her walk to him. They would have a happy life together, he just knew it.

Funny how many townspeople became friendly with Cecily when they heard about the engagement. Even Edith had come around.

Reaching out, he took Cecily's hand, and they stood in front of the judge, reciting their vows. He didn't even wait for the judge to tell him he could kiss the bride. He took her into his arms, stared into her eyes for a moment, and then gave her a very long, passion-filled kiss.

"I love you heart and soul, Shane," she murmured against his lips.

"I'd stopped looking for love until you came along. I love you too, Cecily."

They turned and smiled at the gathering. Asherville was

certainly growing. His friends all appeared happy, but he would bet as the happiest man there.

"It's nice to have so many people to celebrate with, but I'd rather be alone with you," Cecily said as her face grew red.

"Oh, really?"

"Yes, really. I had a long talk with Shannon and Addy. It's not supposed to hurt, you know."

"Is that so?"

"I was thinking we might find out tonight." Her eyes sparkled, and his love for her knew no bounds.

"Have I told you I love you Mrs. O'Connor?"Thank you for taking the time to read Shane's Bride.

THE END

I'm so pleased you chose to read Shane's Bride, and it's my sincere hope that you enjoyed the story. I would appreciate if you'd consider posting a review. This can help an author tremendously in obtaining a readership. My many thanks. ~ Kathleen

ABOUT THE AUTHOR

Sexy Cowboys and the Women Who Love Them...
Finalist in the 2012 and 2015 RONE Awards.
Top Pick, Five Star Series from the Romance Review.
Kathleen Ball writes contemporary and historical western
romance with great emotion and
memorable characters. Her books are award winners and
have appeared on best sellers lists including: Amazon's Best
Seller's List, All Romance Ebooks, Bookstrand, Desert
Breeze Publishing and Secret Cravings Publishing Best
Sellers list. She is the recipient of eight Editor's Choice
Awards, and The Readers' Choice Award for Ryelee's
Cowboy.
Winner of the Lear diamond award Best Historical Novel-
Cinders' Bride
There's something about a cowboy

facebook.com/kathleenballwesternromance

twitter.com/kballauthor

instagram.com/author_kathleenball

OTHER BOOKS BY KATHLEEN

Lasso Spring Series

Callie's Heart

Lone Star Joy

Stetson's Storm

Dawson Ranch Series

Texas Haven

Ryelee's Cowboy

Cowboy Season Series

Summer's Desire

Autumn's Hope

Winter's Embrace

Spring's Delight

Mail Order Brides of Texas

Cinder's Bride

Keegan's Bride

Shane's Bride

Tramp's Bride

Poor Boy's Christmas

Oregon Trail Dreamin'

We've Only Just Begun

A Lifetime to Share

A Love Worth Searching For

So Many Roads to Choose

The Settlers

Greg

Juan

Scarlett

Mail Order Brides of Spring Water

Tattered Hearts

Shattered Trust

Glory's Groom

Battered Soul

The Greatest Gift

Love So Deep

Luke's Fate

Whispered Love

Love Before Midnight

I'm Forever Yours

Finn's Fortune

Glory's Groom

Made in the USA
Monee, IL
31 July 2023